THE HUCKLEBERRY BOOKSHOP

AN ENEMIES TO LOVERS SWEET ROMANCE

HOCKEY SWEETHEARTS
BOOK FIVE

JEAN ORAM

The Huckleberry Bookshop

An Enemies to Lovers Sweet Romance

A Hockey Sweethearts Novel
By Jean Oram

Front cover design by Jess Mastorakos

Complete cataloguing information available online or upon request.

Oram, Jean.

The Huckleberry Bookshop: An Enemies to Lovers Sweet Romance / Jean Oram.—1st. ed.

ISBN: 978-1-990833-63-2, 978-1-990833-64-9, 978-1-990833-65-6 (paperback), 978-1-990833-66-3, 978-1-990833-93-9 (large print), 978-1-990833-62-5 (ebook).

First Oram Productions Edition: April 2025

The
Huckleberry
Bookshop

CHAPTER 1

Athena Gavras wobbled momentarily in her heels, then strode through the ballroom, which was beautifully decorated for the gala. She hadn't gone far when the San Antonio Dragons' publicity agent grabbed her arm.

"Athena!" Nuvella trilled. "I didn't realize you were coming tonight."

"Of course I came. It's a team event." The Dragons had recently started a local charity for sick kids, and everyone on staff had been invited to the Christmas fundraiser. Everyone from the hockey team's dietician—Athena—right on up to the owner, Miranda Fairchild. All rubbing elbows for a good cause. You'd need to have a heart of stone to skip out on tonight. Or a fear of black tie. And Athena had neither.

"I've been meaning to talk to you about the book you're working on." Nuvella arched a perfectly penciled-on eyebrow as she paused, eyeing Athena's vintage couture gown with a curled lip as though considering it severely out of place. And maybe it was—right along with the woman wearing it. But the plum, off-the-shoulder Raffaella Curiel dress with its ruffled, asymmetrical strap looked amazing on her. She felt like she should be lounging on a piano in a smoky club, singing the blues in a husky, sensual voice.

Nuvella couldn't see it, apparently. Or else felt vintage lounge gowns weren't suitable attire at Christmas galas while mingling with millionaire NHL stars.

"*Eat Like a Player*? Is that a working title for your cookbook? Because I don't feel it sends an appropriate message. Perhaps I could recommend a few alternate titles?" She reached for her black-and-white-spotted purse, an unfortunate choice given her nickname, Cruella de Vil, was borne out of her uncanny ability to shred many a soul. That and her bleached hair.

"Sorry, can't chat," Athena said, edging away. She gestured vaguely toward the bar area, assuming she could find at least one player over there breaking her rule about no alcohol during the season. "I've got to talk to the guys."

As the team's dietician, she was the bad guy. It was a role with power, supposedly, but more often than not was nothing short of unrewarding, thanks in large part to center Chadwick Mullens, who all but flaunted his rule-breaking dietary choices.

She wanted to smack him—when she didn't want to kiss that infuriating smirk off his handsome face.

"Remember, we need to keep the Dragons focused on the game, not posing for your cookbook," Nuvella called after her.

Right. The cookbook project that was spiraling out of control due to all the sports egos she'd invited on board. A project she hadn't cleared with the team's head of publicity, Nuvella, who thought it should be all about the Dragons.

Good times.

"It's an official National Hockey League cookbook now,"

Athena replied, sidestepping around a cluster of elegantly dressed mucky-mucks and sending a parting smile over her shoulder. She jumped, finding the woman still hot on her heels. "I only need one or two Dragons."

Athena continued past the orchestra, then several beautifully decorated, sky-high Christmas trees. She aimed herself at the wall of broad shoulders lined up at the bar.

"We need to build up their images…" The publicist's voice faded behind her, blending into the ballroom sounds.

"Who cares about image? We need them to stick to their diets," Athena muttered, marching toward the players.

Just because their somewhat new expansion team was losing, it didn't mean they should throw out her careful, individualized dietary plans. And she'd bet that wide span of tuxedo at the near end of the bar belonged to Chadwick Mullens. He was the ringleader, tempting players away from good habits with his charm, jokes and popularity.

People wanted either to be him or be with him.

Athena approached the high bar, gripped its edge and pulled herself onto a wobbly, vacant wooden stool. The bartender nodded at her.

"Margarita, please."

She lifted a finger, catching herself with an intake of breath. *No alcohol.*

She lowered it and nearly laughed, shaking her head. *She* could drink. She wasn't one of the athletes. But she was so used to lecturing them about their health that she often absorbed the advice herself.

She even cooked out of her first cookbook, a copy of which she'd given to every player on the team.

The man beside her lifted a short glass of amber liquid to his lips.

She knew those lips. Almost daily they smirked at her and indiscriminately allowed any food or drink past them, with no regard to what color list they were on. Green for allowed. Red for off-season only. Orange for moderation.

Athena slid off her stool, ready to scold him, but her stool tipped, dumping her onto her strappy black heels. Her ankle gave way and she crashed against him. Reflexively, a strong, muscled arm snaked around her waist, pressing her to his side, preventing her from tumbling to the parquet flooring. Something cold and wet splashed into her French twist and down her cheek, followed by ice cubes.

"Tina?"

She looked up at the brick wall holding her and shivered as his drink trickled under the edge of her bodice and between her breasts.

Chad Mullens. Sexy wild child. Team bad boy.

And incapable of remembering her real name.

The edge of a tattoo crept up the left side of his neck, peeking above his collar. Just enough was revealed to make her curious. Were those leaves? An angel? A bird? How far did it stretch down his chest? All the way over his hard pecs?

The peek-a-boo tattoo was certainly intentional. He'd probably sketched it out himself, then asked the artist to ink it, anticipating how women would ask about it, giving him an excuse to rip off his shirt and show them. An opportunity to flex those muscles he worked so hard on in the gym. Lifting weights larger than her head like they were fluffy kittens and not hulking weights she could barely budge.

Yes, she'd tried.

Athena cleared her throat, as well as the vision of Chad in a ragged tee, pumping iron, his almost-black locks damp with sweat, the tattoo still frustratingly hidden.

She really needed to stop finding every conceivable excuse to wander past the arena's gym. Because the man was an egomaniac who thought he was too good for her and the Dragons. The type her mother should have warned her about. The type she'd fallen for before.

Never again.

He was bad news in an irresistibly attractive package.

So of course she had a crush on him.

What woman didn't?

And what was it about a brawny, confident man, anyway?

Not her type at all. They were all experienced, Class A heartbreakers.

Man, they were *soooo* her type.

Which meant she needed a new type if she planned to have a still-working heart by age forty.

She coaxed her body to extract itself from Chad's way-too-tempting embrace. Although her steadying left hand seemed unwilling to leave his abs. And her traitorous torso kept cozying closer, her lungs inhaling that amazing after-shave he always wore, which she considered to be his signature scent of seduction.

He was half standing, his solid form pressing against her in the small space between her stool and the bar. His face was level with hers, and with one innocent stumble forward she could lay to rest the fantasy of how it might feel to kiss him.

No.

Find the anger. That shield of righteous indignation.

But his body was so warm against hers. So tempting…

"Chadwick," she said calmly, reminding herself by simply saying his name that he was her enemy.

"Nobody calls me that," he replied, his voice almost gruff. His arms dropped and she wobbled momentarily.

"And my name's not Tina. Does the team doctor need to check your head for brain damage?" She snatched a nearby paper cocktail napkin and dabbed at the side of her face.

His lips twitched at her dig and his gaze swept over her, taking in her gown. The asymmetrical neckline, the vintage skirt. Slinky, sensual. She noted he took a second, quick sweep as though confirming what he'd seen the first time: that the dress made her ample curves scream *va-va-voom*.

"What are you doing here?" he asked.

"I'm part of the team!"

Why did everyone assume that the dietician wouldn't, or couldn't, come to the black-tie fundraiser? Did they think she didn't exist outside her small office in the bowels of the arena? She had a life beyond the Dragons. A big, busy life! She was constantly creating new recipes in her mother's kitchen for her cookbooks and the players, and would soon open a bookstore with her sister.

She was plenty busy. They were lucky she could even make it tonight.

She snatched a stack of napkins from the bar and swiped them down the beads of moisture on Chad's retro tuxedo. Damn, he wore it well. Not many people could get away with wearing something so painfully out of style. And yet instead of laughing at his ruffled, baby blue tuxedo shirt she was almost drooling over his wide chest and daydreaming of pirates and wanton escapades.

"Are you—" his eyes narrowed "—petting me?"

Her attention snapped upward. His charming smirk was aimed directly at her, hitting like a solar flare to the gut.

"No," she said breathlessly. "I'm saving this relic you call an outfit. Who knows what that drink might do to the fabric." *Let alone your body's ability to perform in tomorrow night's game.*

She glared at him and dabbed at her wet cheek and collarbone. The liquid smelled fruity. Apple-spiced whiskey, perhaps? Bold choice.

"Are you trying to get me to notice you, Tina?" he asked, leaning a bit too close. His deep, rough growl was like dirty sex, ripping the oxygen from her lungs. "Falling on me... petting me."

How did he always manage to make every room feel so hot? Chadwick Mullens was the true cause of global warming.

"I'm wearing heels, *Chad*. I never wear high heels. I mean, I do sometimes. But not very often, because they can be really bad for a person's feet." She cleared her throat, telling her nerves to take a hike. His flirting was not personal. He used it as a universal get-out-of-jail-free card, and she was impervious.

You hear that, uterus and other lady bits? Impervious.

"I'm wearing heels tonight, and I forgot when I got off this stupidly tall stool which is incredibly unstable." She gave the seat an angry flick and, as though to prove her words, it tipped over, knocking into Daisy-Mae Ray, the team captain's girlfriend.

"Oh, I'm so sorry!" Athena scurried to retrieve the seat, cringing as Daisy-Mae eyed Chad, then mouthed to her, *"Are you okay?"*

She nodded quickly as Chad brushed her side, reaching past her to right the stool with one strong hand. He set it at the bar and gripped Athena's elbow, ready to help her climb onto her perch again. "Join us?"

She took in the row of men. They'd all turned to see what was happening behind them. Noting they'd gained her attention, they swiveled away, their shoulders angled as though hiding something. She leaned over the bar to peer at the whiskey glasses sitting in front of them.

"Are you *all* drinking tonight?" Unable to help it, she gasped in outrage. "No wonder you boys can't grab a win. You're not following my diet plans at all!"

"Don't tell Athena," one of the men down the way muttered. Others chuckled under their breath.

She was a joke. The uptight, no-fun, uncool mother hen.

That hurt more than it should.

Her margarita arrived and she sucked back a mouthful of the lime-green slush, then set the glass down when the sudden cold tightened her temples. If her team didn't want to win, why should she care? Why was she working harder for their goals than they were? They earned their millions whether they won or lost.

Another drop of Chad's drink dribbled down her cheek, and Athena licked the side of her mouth. Apple-something for sure. Hard to tell, as it was a bit watered down from the melting ice.

Truly, what did it matter? Chad was boozing it up as if her degree in nutrition and dietetics was a farce.

He offered her a fresh napkin, batting his lashes and, if she didn't know any better, looking surprisingly chagrinned.

She snatched it and dabbed at her face. "If y'all don't want to win, then what's the point of me even trying?"

He shot her that devilish get-out-of-jail-free smile.

She balled up the napkin and tossed it at his chest. "Know what, Chadwick Raul Mullens? Joke's on you because I quit."

* * *

"Don't quit." Mullens snagged Athena's arm, preventing her from storming off.

Irritation flickered in her hazel eyes as she glanced pointedly at his hand. He released her.

"We're not worth it," he said.

"I know."

"Then why—"

"I do my best to avoid expending energy in exercises of futility."

"I love it when you use that sexy vocabulary of yours."

"Chadwick..." Her tone held a warning.

Why did it wreck him every time she used his first name? Nobody called him Chad, and nobody but the government and medical professionals ever referred to him as Chadwick.

And yet hearing her say his name, even when laced with barely constrained hostility, tumbled every carefully constructed boulder that made his public persona and left him there as nothing more than a man with a crush on a really smart woman he wasn't sure how to relate to. She had an exterior made of Kevlar and his charms never managed a penetrating hit. And his charms were all he had.

It didn't help that he'd completely blown the first impression he'd made on her. Blown it like he'd metaphorically handed her a live grenade after lighting fire to everything she held dear.

"Don't take us seriously. We're just a bunch of useless jocks," he said.

Her lips pursed and her spine straightened.

This was the first time he'd seen that the guys flaunting her rules might actually get under her skin. Tonight there was no good-natured eye-rolling or shaking of her head. She was mad. Actually mad.

Mullens glanced back at his teammates, unable to explain why tonight felt so different. There was something fragile about the players' spirits. They'd lost so badly and so repeatedly over the past two months. That did things to a man, especially when they were on the league's last-chance team and more losses might threaten their careers.

"We've barely won a game all season," he said quietly. "There's a lot of steam to be blown off."

"Maybe if you tried following the diet plan—no sugar, no *alcohol*—you might have better results." She raised an eyebrow at the line of men hunched over their drinks, sipping furtively. Her large, dark eyes lifted to Mullens' own and he felt caught out. Busted as the worst offender. The ringleader. The one whose attitude gave everyone implicit consent to blow her off.

It was all he could do not to look away in shame.

"We need someone busting our chops," he muttered.

"Then call your moms."

Unable to help it, he flinched. "Imagine how bad it would be if we didn't have you."

"Well, let's see. I'd be happier. Stress-free." She lifted her arms, her face softening into a smile as though she was imagining herself on a beach somewhere. "Sounds like a win to me."

He'd never get back on a real team if she gave up on them. He'd be stuck here until there was nothing left to salvage. Gone and forgotten.

She was the only thing between him and being a failure.

In the split second Mullens had spent mulling over his potential personal losses, Athena had escaped. He put down his empty glass and hustled after the flash of plum-and-black fabric. Past the full dance floor and out the tall ballroom door that was just swinging shut again.

She was moving fast, her sexy gown swishing around her calves.

"Tina!"

She strode faster.

He snagged her elbow before she hit the ladies' room across from the ballroom, but she did some sort of grip-breaking move that freed her. She vanished through the doorway and he followed.

"Tina."

She whirled, her mouth dropping open, her voice shaking. "Get out!"

He stepped toward her and she stumbled backward in surprise, hitting the sink counter with her hip before backing against the room's far wall.

"The team needs you," he insisted, planting himself in front of her.

"I *know*." Her cheeks were pink and her chest heaved as though she'd just finished a sprint.

"So you can't quit because of me." He placed one palm on the patterned tile beside her, needing to steady himself against the subtle scent of her cocoa butter lotion, not to mention their intoxicating closeness.

She crossed her arms, ensuring there was space between them. She glared up at him with lips that looked way too kissable. "Give me one good reason not to."

"We need you to get us back on real teams," he said without thinking. "Or at least help us turn this one into a winner so we don't lose everything we've spent our lives working toward."

She scoffed. "Maybe if you followed the diet plan, you'd be

a winning team." She gave him a shove, then darted around him as he regained his equilibrium.

"I wasn't traded because of my food choices, Tina."

"Yeah? Then why were you?" She turned, her tone mocking. "Sleep with the wrong woman? Sorry. *Women.*"

He felt the tendons in his jaw ping as he clamped his teeth together. That had totally been offside. He hadn't even been on a date—of any kind—in months.

And as for why he'd been traded? He still had no clue. None. He'd thought he'd been doing great, a rising star, and then suddenly here he was on the lowest ranking team, looking at the possible end of the only life he knew.

"Maybe..." she stalked closer, eyes narrowed "...you got traded because of your ego and rotten attitude and inability to follow rules." She gave his chest a sharp tap.

He placed a hand over the spot where she'd made contact. "No need to be mean about it."

"I learned from the best—you."

He grabbed her hand, keeping her near while he considered his next words. His long-overdue apology.

Instead, like a bad habit, he dropped his voice and said, low and sexy, "And yet you haven't learned the good stuff, such as breaking the rules, letting loose and having a little fun."

Mullens shot her a playful smile. He knew she could be fun. He'd caught her in rare moments—usually laughing with another player (which ended abruptly as soon as he appeared) —when her face was awash with joy, her spirit so big it filled the room.

She stared at him, her lips moving slightly as though she was choosing which comeback to lob his way.

He cupped her hand in both of his, raising it between them. "Why do you hate me, Tina?"

"How much time do you have?"

He chuckled.

She narrowed her eyes. "Is this all some big joke to you?"

He shrugged.

"Skating around, pulling in millions for knocking into other millionaires? I guess, really…how is that not a joke?" She leaned in, her tone soft, her lips shiny from her gloss. She'd done something different with her eye shadow, and he found himself caught in her beautiful depths. "Some of us work really hard to make you and the team look good, and you blow us off like entitled, elitist jerks. And for us mere humans, that hurts."

When her eyes welled up, his heart sank.

"Please don't quit." he told her.

"Why shouldn't I?"

"We need you."

"You're going to have to do better than that, because I don't owe you anything." She pulled her hand free and walked to the door.

Mullens sighed and ran his fingers through his hair, doubting himself.

She was going to make him say it.

But what was "it," exactly?

That he actually followed her plan when nobody was looking? That he didn't know why he'd been traded, but worried that her comment about ego was accurate? That he was secretly panicked that he might be stuck on this losing expansion team for the rest of his now-fizzling career?

He'd never admit to that. Never crack the façade of his carefully cultivated image.

He was a confident man in charge of his own damn castle.

But she was well beyond allowing him that thin edge of forgiveness he thrived upon. That small caving in that he could leverage into full-blown amnesia where his faults were concerned. In other words, there was no BS-ing this woman, even though he'd pulled the wool over her eyes with how he fueled his body.

He watched her tug open the door and step through, a sensuous compilation of curves and temptation.

He had to say something.

Anything.

The door closed behind her.

CHAPTER 2

"*Y*ou didn't quit."

It was Monday afternoon and Chadwick Mullens stood in Athena's office doorway, one thick, muscled shoulder pressing into the doorjamb.

Athena'd had a feeling he'd appear at some point today, but not to apologize for Friday's drinking at the gala. Any time a player missed an appointment with her—or the team's physical therapist—the managers and coaches heard about it. As a result, she had very few no-shows, even if the men didn't always follow her advice or their personalized meal plans.

And since Chad was no longer in her calendar—thanks to her removal of him—the word had likely reached their head coach, and therefore gotten back to Chad.

You mess with the bull, you're going to get the horns. Merry Christmas, Chadwick.

Athena continued working, ignoring the sting of guilt she felt for her bold move in having him taken off her roster. A few years ago she'd never have had the guts. But now that she was in her thirties? Well, she had a new confidence in herself, her skills, and also in how she expected to be treated.

Living with a hockey player—even for only five months—had taught her a lot.

She studiously kept her focus on tweaking the formatting for a gluten-free recipe, ready to defend her position on removing him from her appointment book. Unlike Chad, the player who'd requested the recipe was fully on board with taking care of his health and building his strength in order to contribute to the team. No matter what.

Maybe it was because he was responsible for a family. Or maybe his wife figured that, for the sake of sanity, the family of five would all eat the same meals. Which meant they ate gluten-free to accommodate their seven-year-old celiac son, something Athena was more than happy to incorporate when sharing recipes to go with the man's dietary plan.

Maybe that was what Chad needed to whip him into shape —a family. Things changed when you were responsible for others, and a wife and kids might offer a little motivation to alter his self-centered actions and toe the line.

"What are you snorting about?" he asked.

"Imagining you as a dad."

She adjusted the spacing on the digital document and sent it to her printer.

"What? Why?" He jerked upright in the doorway.

She rolled her eyes and took a sip of her sweetened huckleberry tea.

"You pregnant?" His tone went softer, more seductive, undoubtedly with the intention of melting her undergarments. Little did he know hers were made of high-quality steel and were unmeltable by the likes of him. "Because I've heard I can get a woman in the family way with just one look. Never had a chance to prove it until now."

She sprayed the mouthful of tea back into her cup and started coughing.

Grinning, Chad took that as an invitation, entering the room and settling into the chair opposite her desk.

Eyes watering, Athena spun in her chair to grab the papers from her whirling printer. A stack of boxes was in the way, so she stood and moved a heavy carton of books aside, then snatched the recipes, tucking one into the player's folder and the extra into a folder for her NHL cookbook project.

Chad had made himself comfortable and was grinning at her confidently while man-spreading in the chair across from her desk. Worse, he sported that wicked, unpredictable twitch of his lips where she never knew what he was going to say next.

"Did you need something?" she snapped. It was becoming clear that he hadn't heard from the coach. Which meant he'd be visiting her office a second time this week. And that was twice more than she could handle.

"Maybe you did quit." He leaned forward, squinting at the text on one of the boxes taking over her space. "Moving out?"

"You wish."

She dropped into her chair, guiltily silencing her cell phone, which chirped with an incoming call from her mom. Darianna was having another tough day, her multiple sclerosis flaring up, and Athena had promised to get a grocery list from her. Her dad could run out, but Athena felt better having him at home when her mom was going through a rough patch. Plus she quite enjoyed grocery shopping, and her father always forgot one or two key items on the list.

"New cookbooks for us to take home?" Chad asked, gesturing to the boxes.

"To use as doorstops? Not a chance."

"Coordinating another food drive for hungry kids?"

She crossed her arms, glancing at the boxes, hoping he couldn't read the labels from where he sat. To save a few bucks, as well as hassles over signing for the deliveries, she'd used her work address instead of her future bookstore's. Next month the Huckleberry Bookshop would open in her hometown of Sweetheart Creek, a dream she and her sister Medora—Meddy—had clung to for years. Now it was happening. And so she now had an office filled with heavy boxes, several floors away from her parked car.

She was going to have biceps that rivaled Chad's by the time the shop was open.

"Did you need something?" Athena repeated, finally daring to look directly at him. His big brown eyes were rimmed with long black lashes that always made her think of a little boy, rather than the chiseled athlete with tattoos and a stance that said he was all man—and that he'd fight anyone who suggested otherwise. There was something in those eyes that drew her in and caused her to be fond of him without reason.

And that was a problem.

"You can't quit, Tina."

"You think irritating me is cute, don't you?"

He grinned again.

The day she answered to "Tina" was the day he'd win.

Never happening. She'd rather give up cooking and reading—her two favorite hobbies.

"When's your last day?"

"Who said I'm quitting?"

"You did."

"After you tossed your whiskey on me, despite the—"

"I didn't!" He sat up, the casual vibe gone from his loose limbs.

"Fine! Scotch! Rye! Whatever it was!"

"I was *catching* you."

"You were getting rid of the evidence!" She stood, her breath coming fast and hard.

He scowled, standing as well.

She pressed a finger against her desk's surface. "Just because you don't listen to my advice doesn't mean others on the team don't still value me—despite your best efforts." She waved the folder of recipes as validation.

"You take yourself too seriously."

"And you don't take your privileged career seriously enough!"

He perched on the edge of her desk, his expression dark, his jaw tight. He inhaled slowly, the anger falling away, the cavalier ease returning. He smiled, and it felt similar to a blast of spring sunshine after a long bitter winter. Whoever had told him he was dead sexy with those eyes of his did the rest of womankind a serious disservice. The man wielded them like a weapon.

Well, she had one, too.

"I've removed your appointments from my schedule. Eat and drink whatever you want. You're now free of my ineffective bimonthly nagging."

The smile dropped. "You didn't."

"Of course I did. Why would I force you to do somothing you hate?" She tossed the folder onto a stack of boxes and flashed him a deceptively sweet smile.

"You're going to ruin my career? Over one drink? One I didn't even get to enjoy before you decided to bathe in it?"

"Chadwick Mullens," she said sternly, leaning toward him across her small desk, "you made the choice. Repeatedly. It's clear you don't care."

"Tina… Come on."

"I'm curious, though." She gestured to the wider world beyond the arena. "This is all good enough for you—what you have? You no longer feel the need to invest in your future? You have so much that you can safely sabotage a few years?"

His eyes dropped to the wide silver rings lining his fingers.

"It almost seems as though this might all be too good for you, Chadwick. Like you feel it's more than you deserve."

"Sorry. Did I step into the team shrink's office?" He leaned back, squinting at the sign on her open office door.

"You know, some of the guys on the team care. A lot. They want more and you're holding them back by acting like a spoiled teenager." She pushed back from the desk, stepped toward the door and pulled it wide. "Now if you'll excuse me, I have a call with my publisher."

He slid his frame from her desk. "Publisher?"

"Oh, right. You probably thought that cookbook I gave you at the beginning of the season was a gag gift. It's actually a bestseller, and surprise, surprise, they have me writing another one." She patted his arm as he blinked at her from the doorway. "I'm sure your agent deleted your invitation to join the project, since we're all well aware that the link between dietary choices and performance isn't something you subscribe to."

She smiled and shut the door, feeling only slightly bad about his wounded expression.

Just slightly.

* * *

Her publisher.

Second cookbook.

Mullens stared at the Christmas wreath on Athena's closed door and rubbed his jaw. He'd forgotten to shave in his rush to get to the rink before she was done for the day. She worked odd hours and was off-site frequently enough that he never knew where she'd be or when.

She thought he didn't want more from his career and that he was sabotaging himself.

He muttered a curse, thinking of the corner he'd painted himself into. It had started on his first day during the dietary orientation for new players. He'd been eager to strut his stuff, and show everyone he didn't belong on the low-ranked team and that he wouldn't be there for long. He'd work hard, be a star and get traded somewhere good by the end of season.

But then practically the first words out of Athena Gavras's mouth had hit him right in the core. Inadvertently allowing his tamped down memories of pain and loneliness to resurface.

Those damn pancakes. The last family meal before it all fell apart.

He was not going to think about it.

She had looked straight at him with those kind eyes and her sweetness had shot straight into his hurting soul. Then she'd put him on the spot and he'd reacted. Without thinking, he'd made a choice. Reveal this vulnerability in front of his new teammates, or crack a joke—at her expense?

Because he was a hockey player, in a room filled with other jocks, he'd chosen the latter. He'd chosen survival.

He'd made her rules and recipes the butt of a joke that had immediately solidified his image with this team as a devil-may-care rule-breaker.

He wanted a do-over.

There was something about Athena Gavras that ripped him open. It was as though all the stuff he'd jammed inside, hidden behind concrete walls and forgotten about, tumbled out whenever she was around. He hated that sensation of the earth sliding out from underfoot. The balancing he had to do around her. One step too far and he'd be at her feet, raw and vulnerable. One step in the other direction and she'd never speak to him again.

He sucked in a slow breath and forced himself to walk away from her office. He needed to find Coach Louis and explain the whole off-the-dietician's-roster situation.

Hey, Louis, man. Yeah, this hiccup with Athena? It's just a personality conflict. But I'm following the plan, so no big deal if I skip the appointments, right?

The problem was that once he'd made a show of giving her attitude, it had become a thing—his thing. Nobody would believe he secretly followed her nutrition guidance to a T. Not even Coach.

Athena should have cut him from her appointment book months ago.

Mullens mulled over his problem as he headed deeper into the arena, toward Louis's office.

He pulled out his phone and dialed his agent.

"What's Athena Gavras working on with her publisher? And how do I get in on it?"

"Pretty sure that window's closed," Rafard replied, unfazed by Mullens' abruptness.

"She said I was invited."

"Small fish. Not your thing."

That sounded similar to something he may have parroted

to Rafard. Or maybe his agent knew him well and was preemptively striking deals without telling him about them?

The man did work closely with Mullens' business manager, and some weeks an overwhelming amount of proposals flew back and forth among the three of them. It wouldn't be unreasonable to leave Mullens out of the loop from time to time.

"What's it called?" he asked.

"Let me see if I can find it." The sound of fingers dancing over a keyboard came through his phone. "Here we go. From late September. It went out to the whole team. *The NHL cookbook: Eat like a Player*. You said no."

"Right. Well, I want to be on the cover. Or inside it. In the commercials. Whatever she needs."

"This isn't your brand." His agent's tone turned dismissive. "And the pay is literally peanuts. It's not what you're looking for in terms of financial incentive or visibility."

"Get me on the cover."

"Not your image," Rafard stated curtly.

"So make the book my image."

"It's her project," he replied patiently. "Not yours. And as for your image, we've worked really hard on it for years. It's not going anywhere. And certainly not for some cookbook."

Mullens pinched the bridge of his nose. He needed time with Athena. Not only because she was curvy and gorgeous and he couldn't figure out how to get her to like him. But also because he needed her help to save his career. Possibly literally.

Showing her a little respect would probably be a good start....

"I need to play nice with her."

"She knocked up?"

"No," he replied sharply. Man, his business manager really had done a bang-up job of cementing Mullens' image. For the past several years he'd loved it. At the moment, though, not so much. He sighed. "Just make it happen, Rafard."

He hung up and rounded the last corner to the coach's office.

What was he going to do? His usual charm didn't work on Athena. He'd called her bluff, and she'd struck—hard.

He loved her for it, even though it created a pit of fear in his stomach. How could she, the team's dietician, hold such important cards? And why couldn't he have just kept his head down and his mouth shut the day they'd met? Why had he reacted like such an unstable teenaged boy?

He reached Louis's dark office and tried the handle. Locked. Ever since Coach had moved back to Sweetheart Creek he was barely around. Rumor was he had his heart set on some chick from his past.

But Louis? The idea of him forsaking work to chase some gal was almost laughable. The whole thing about the woman was likely just that—a rumor.

Mullens' phone rang. It was Rafard.

"That was fast."

"Dude, don't hang up on me."

"Sorry."

"I need to know what you're willing to offer."

"What do you mean?"

"A carrot. For the publisher. Something big to get you in on this project—assuming it hasn't already gone to print."

"It hasn't." He hoped. "Give her whatever she needs."

Athena would see right through his ploy to get into her cookbook, but it was the best plan he had.

"And Rafard? Tell her my proceeds will go toward feeding hungry kids."

CHAPTER 3

"What? Say that again?" Athena frowned at her phone. Her literary agent's words made no sense.

"His agent called. He wants to be on the cover. Merry Christmas! Your book is going to sell crazy amounts with that hunk gracing its pages. Say hello to big money in the New Year!"

Athena rubbed her forehead and scrunched her eyes shut, pacing the crowded back room of her shop on Main Street, Sweetheart Creek. She had too much on her plate at the moment to even think about Chad Mullens elbowing his way into her project.

Case in point, she—a dietician—had just sent her sister across the street for greasy takeout because she—who lived in one of the two apartments above the shop—had nothing in her fridge. (Neither did her sister, who lived in the second apartment, but Meddy wasn't paid to provide people with the tools and skills to eat nutritiously.) Right now Athena was supposed to be clearing off an eating space in the former café's old kitchen, not on the phone. Not worrying about a huge personality taking over *her* cookbook.

She nudged a box aside and blinked away tears of fatigue and frustration. One month until the Huckleberry Bookshop's grand opening. One month and a day, to be exact. And it looked as though they'd need at least three months to pull it all together.

"I know we already settled on the cover," Aurora was saying. Athena peered into an abandoned coffee cup, debating if the latte was too old and cold to drink. She tucked the phone between her ear and shoulder and picked up another box of books, carrying it to the storage area at the back of the building. "But…Mullens? Hottie McHot Hot. So, what do you say? Happy Hanukkah? Are you Jewish? Or maybe I should say happy Chinese New Year?" There was a short pause. "Because I said this wouldn't be a problem."

Athena almost dropped her phone as she headed back to the kitchen to collect another load of books.

"But he doesn't fit the image!" Never mind all the weeks of fighting she'd endured to get a beautiful book cover that would now be scrapped. Because in walks Chadwick Mullens and he was going to be on it instead. It was like putting a cup of white sugar on the cover of a sugar-free cookbook.

"Um," Aurora said, her voice filled with amusement, "your book is called *Eat Like a Player*. He's a player—in both senses of the word. We both know he's perfect."

That's what she'd thought the first time she'd met him, too. Perfect. Until she'd actually tried to do her job and discovered that he was a jerk. It still smarted how she'd fallen for the way he'd leaned in. He'd leaned toward her as though she was interesting, gorgeous and intriguing. Like he didn't want to miss a word.

She'd been so excited to welcome the new players to the team and to share some of her favorite recipes. Chad had been sitting close to the front, the tattoo that peeked above his collar drawing her eyes, his wide silver rings somehow the sexiest thing she'd seen on a man in eons. He hadn't shaved that morning and was looking rugged, yet still put together in his crisp, striped shirt and bold tie with dark jeans. The man had been as delicious as the vegetarian enchilada recipe she'd just perfected the night before.

She'd felt the connection with him when she introduced herself to the room. And then he'd leaned in.

Leaned in.

And all her brain's warnings about him being a player among the ladies had gone right out the window.

She'd had his attention, and for whatever asinine reason, her biochemistry had embraced that heady feeling and made her consider falling in love all over again. Or at least lust.

She was such a sucker. She'd thought she'd seen something in the way he'd tuned in to her talk, as though he understood the dietary language she was speaking. Feeling emboldened—stupid heady feelings—she'd cracked a joke about the difference between boogers and broccoli.

He'd replied instantly with the punch line that kids didn't eat broccoli. Then he'd given her a ghost of a smile and pulled back, locking her out of that irresistible connection they'd been enjoying.

Okay, okay, so sometimes she wasn't cool or sexy. She was a bit of a book nerd and a rule follower. And immature. Because who told booger jokes to a roomful of hot jocks?

Aware she'd put him off, she'd focused on her talk, babbling about a favorite recipe. Walnut carrot pancakes that were low glycemic and hearty. Great for an athlete looking for a sharp carb increase, but not an accompanying spike in sugar levels. But the more she talked, the tighter his jaw got. Feeling she was losing him, and therefore probably all the other players in the room, she'd decided to get personal. She'd told them about her family's game night and how they made breakfast for supper those nights, and that the pancake recipe with all the toppings were their all-time favorite.

She'd then grabbed the stack of recipes and turned to him, worried about the flexing in his jaw. "Chadwick?" she'd said softly, handing him a recipe. "Do you want carrot pancakes?"

The sheet wavered in the air between them.

"Chad?"

He'd snatched the page and crumpled it, dropping it onto the table in front of him, jaw so tight she worried about his molars.

"I don't do pancakes."

And that had been it. The atmosphere had changed, the fun sucked from her talk, a tone set that she couldn't ever quite undo.

* * *

"You don't want a good-looking, recognizable pro hockey player on the cover of your cookbook for athletes?" Aurora asked Athena, steering her thoughts away from Memory Lane and back to the problem at hand.

"No, I do." She just didn't want *him*. If she'd wanted a player on the front, she could have found one.

"His face will sell tons of copies," her agent said. Her tone suggested the paperwork with Chad had already been signed by the publisher and the call was mere courtesy.

"So, he's going to be on the cover?"

"And we're going to fit him into your marketing plan."

"My marketing plan?" Realizing she sounded like a petulant preschooler, Athena sucked in a deep breath.

Seriously though? She'd tried cutting the belligerent rule-breaker from her life and now here he was back in full force like an infestation.

He'd done this on purpose.

He'd done this to show her who was boss, who held the cards.

Damn him, but she kind of respected the audacity of his crafty ploy.

"Fine," she said carefully, shaking her head at the predicament of her own making. "What do you have in mind?"

"You'd pitched a YouTube cooking channel in your book proposal. They're setting that up for you as we speak."

"But it was nixed." Athena dropped a box of books near the back door in frustration, then gripped her phone tighter and stretched her neck while she returned for another load. "They told me I don't have the right flair to be an online personality."

Her phone beeped with an incoming call. Her dad. She ignored it, making a mental note to call him back.

"Mullens is on board," Aurora said, "and so is the marketing department so they've decided to go ahead with it."

"He doesn't even cook!" Didn't someone have to clear these kinds of marketing changes with her since they involved her?

"You'll teach him. He'll bring the celebrity and you'll bring the cooking skills. You'll act as foils to each other. But don't go to the extreme. You'll need to lighten up and be fun."

"I am light and fun."

Well, she used to be. Before life got so serious. There were only so many if-it-doesn't-kill-you kind of experiences a woman could take before they dampened her sunshiny optimism.

"Marketing is sending you a filming coach. The publisher is fully on board with all of this." There was a hint of warning in Aurora's voice.

"What's a filming coach?"

Her phone beeped again with another incoming call. Her dad, Neandro, again.

"His name's Howell. He'll critique your on-camera personality. Give you tips and all of that so you're not overshadowed by Mullens. He'll help you develop your personal brand, and we'll steer you away from anything too bookish and inaccessible personality-wise. Okay? Nothing boring. All dazzle-dazzle sunshine and entertaining fun."

Athena stared around the bookstore's back room and the towers of boxes surrounding her. Nothing bookish? And was her agent calling her boring and no fun?

Was Chad right? Did she take herself too seriously? Was she creating barriers between herself and others with her seriousness and drive?

She used to be fun. Used to laugh.

Or maybe she was just hanging out with the wrong people and they simply didn't appreciate her bookishness and found it all a bit boring.

She shook her head. Spending time with hockey players and publishers was getting to her. She was fine. She was accomplishing amazing things with her life.

Even if she was a bit overwhelmed by the idea of suddenly having to create a few meals in front of a camera, plus developing her own *brand*. It was the biggest challenge she'd yet to face.

Did she even have time for this?

Putting together a second cookbook was supposed to be a fast and easy project, but was quickly becoming a third job. Or was it her fourth? She was team dietician, something she could do in her sleep. She was starting a business with her younger sister, which was a bit out of either of their depths. She'd just finished creating recipes for the new cookbook—tested on the team, of course—and now had to build herself an online personality?

But a cooking show. She really wanted that.

She'd even play nice with Mr. Hot Stuff Playboy in order to get it.

Not that she'd ever tell Chadwick Mullens she *needed* him.

"Howell will come by tomorrow. We'd like you to use recipes from both cookbooks."

"But tomorrow is Christmas Eve!" Athena sputtered. She had plans to bake traditional Greek goodies with her mom and sister, inhale the wonderful aroma of Christmas thanks to the fresh pine in the living room that was straight from Cassandra McTavish's local Christmas tree lot, and shift into low gear for a few days.

How had all this video stuff been arranged so quickly? Was this how fast events moved when a celebrity got involved in a project? Everything kicked into a supersonic speed, as if the producers were afraid the celeb would move on if given half a beat to breathe or think—or forget about it and renege?

Although she had a few other NHL players penciled in for some promos in January and February—just before the book's March launch—and nobody had been moving this fast with them. Maybe this was the special "Mullens Effect?"

"So Howell is going to come by your kitchen," Aurora said, and Athena glanced around the disaster zone. She'd believed she had weeks, not hours, to whip the dusty kitchen into shape before the grand opening. However, she had listed it as the available commercial kitchen in her online video pitch to her publisher, and she couldn't suddenly say she didn't have access to it anymore. Maybe she could enlist her family and friends to help out. They'd do almost anything in exchange for a batch of her fresh-baked brownies.

"He'll critique you," Aurora continued, "and make sure the dynamic between you and Mullens really pops."

"I don't think that'll be a concern," Athena muttered. "There will be a murder mystery dinner in each and every episode."

Her agent laughed. "The marketing department will iron out the details of your theme. If you can get some of his favorite recipes, or ones that are favorites in his family, that would be great. Really involve him on all levels, so he's not just a marketing ploy."

Which he was.

The man was calling her bluff and trying to get her to ease up on tattling to Louis about his diet. After all, she'd threatened to take away what was dear to him, and now he was initiating payback. She couldn't fault him for that. She would have done the same in his position.

Meddy barged through the kitchen door, waving a bag of wonderfully scented takeout and causing Athena's stomach to growl. Her sister's phone was wedged between her ear and shoulder and she was saying loudly, "No, Dad, we didn't forget tonight is FBGN." She turned her rounded eyes to Athena.

Family Breakfast Game Night. *That's* why Athena hadn't grocery shopped. The four of them would binge all night, and she and Meddy, despite any protestations on their part, would surely come home with leftovers. She'd forgotten about FBGN since it was only two days until Christmas.

Game night started with carrot-walnut pancakes, sausage, fresh fruit and scrambled eggs. Then came several ruthless rounds of cutthroat cards. It had been a tradition since the day Meddy had come home from kindergarten upset that she didn't know her numbers as well as the top kids in her class. Their dad had instituted a family game night on the spot, with playing cards at the center, finding a fun way for her to get better at her numbers. It had been such a blast it had become an instant, unbreakable tradition.

Until Athena moved to Jersey to live with Lonnie a little over a year ago. She'd missed family game night as she sat alone with Lonnie's cat, Banx, waiting for him to come home from hockey.

But five months later—early last spring—she'd been single and back in Sweetheart Creek again, with a position with the Dragons and no longer taking family time for granted. And in September, when her sister had been downsized from the county office, they'd pooled their savings and bought the shop, including the two apartments above.

"Of course we'll be there." Meddy cringed dramatically and checked her watch. She mouthed to Athena, *"Thirty minutes."*

They were going to have to inhale their takeout. Athena tucked her phone between her cheek and shoulder, making gimme hands at the bag. She was rewarded with a wrapped, hot cheeseburger.

She was lucky she wasn't a pro athlete, for she'd never make it a week following the strict diet she gave them. Then again, nobody was offering her a million or two a year to stay in top physical shape. And anyway, she allowed her players the odd binge day, which was what takeout from the Longhorn Diner was, right?

And on the odd chance that the greasy cheeseburger didn't count, then chasing it down with a second supper over at her parents' surely would.

She mouthed *"Thanks"* to Meddy, set the burger on the mostly cleared counter and began unwrapping it with her free hand, making sounds of agreement into her phone as Aurora continued to talk, going over their publishing schedule.

"But back to Chad Mullens," Athena finally said. "How's he getting paid for this?"

If she recalled correctly, her publisher had a flat fee payable to any stars who joined the project. But knowing the savvy Mr. Mullens, he'd probably leveraged something extra. "Is he taking a cut of the royalties or making extra sponsorship deals on top of this?"

"Just the flat fee, which he's donating to a hungry kids' charity."

Athena paused over her burger and closed her eyes, holding back a growl. A food-related charity? For kids?

He really was playing hardball, and planning to strike her out by aiming straight for her heartstrings.

She dropped her cheeseburger on the counter, no longer famished, and asked, "Is there any possible way I can say no?"

* * *

"Anyone here?" Mullens asked, opening the back door of an empty building on Main Street, Sweetheart Creek. The front windows were papered over and the front door locked. A handwritten sign suggested the place was soon going to be a bookstore and café and that deliveries would be accepted around back between certain hours.

Double-checking the address given to him by Athena's publishing team yesterday, he'd left his gorgeous, factory-ordered, volcano-gray metallic Porsche parked out front and walked around to the alley, wondering if Athena was having a laugh at his expense. He'd considered driving away, but was already on thin ice with Louis and the Dragons' managers because of his rift with the dietician. And even though it had been confirmed that the coach was falling for some local chick, that didn't mean he'd go easy on Mullens.

What if this address snafu was retribution? Athena wasn't one to ignore a battle cry, and he'd pushed his way into her cookbook project. She could be sending him to an abandoned building in a charming town of less than five thousand people, with plans to lock him inside so he'd miss Christmas. The joke was on her; he didn't have anywhere to be tomorrow.

Mullens didn't see Athena as that vindictive and cruel, though. And involving her publishing team in a prank against him was too likely to backfire on her. Plus he had a cell phone, and could call for help, foiling her plan.

He shook off his paranoia and eased through the building's rear door, allowing his eyes to adjust to the limited light in the windowless space. His agent had been quick, with barely forty-eight hours passing between Mullens' get-me-in-the-cookbook request and now wondering if he was in the right place to shoot a cooking video.

A cooking video with Athena Gavras. Boy, was that ever a mine field.

He focused on getting his head back in the game. Time to play nice, give her a peace offering, woo the camera and win the day.

Hearing voices, and spotting a shaft of light coming from a room up ahead, he wove through a maze of stacked boxes, wondering if hoarders ever felt claustrophobic.

The well-lit room turned out to be a kitchen.

Athena had her back to him and was wearing a lightweight, hot pink sweater that clung to her generous curves. Her shiny brown locks hung loose over her shoulders. He'd bet she had the softest hair, similar to that model he'd dated on and off during his rookie season.

A bright light and tripoded camera were positioned across the counter from where she was standing, a stove and a doorway to the back storage area at her back. A slender man with a goatee was lecturing her on loosening up and making the camera her friend.

"Hey, am I late?" Mullens asked, shrugging out of his Dragons jacket. As requested by the team's PR demon-lady he was wearing a Dragons jersey for the video. Nuvella had called him earlier that morning reminding him about wardrobe, as well as the small fact that he'd be representing his team in these videos. In other words, behave.

Athena turned toward him, her jaw tight. "I thought we weren't doing team paraphernalia."

He set the gift he'd brought her on the edge of the counter, grabbed the hem of his jersey and began peeling it off.

Nuvella stood up from where she'd been perched on a box in the corner, commanding, "Jersey *and* hat, Mullens." Her voice was even firmer as she turned to Athena. "I made it clear."

"No hats," said the man by the camera.

Mullens paused, the shirt half off.

"This isn't a Dragons thing," Athena argued. "No jersey."

"Hats cause too many shadows."

"Jersey on, Mullens."

He dropped his team colors back over his T-shirt and shot Athena a wry look, but her head was down, her lips pressed in a firm line.

"Let's have you over here." The man with the goatee grabbed Mullens' arm and steered him to the other side of the counter, stopping him beside Athena. "Pretend to cook something and I'll critique."

Eggs, mushrooms, spinach, shredded broccoli crowns and cheese—probably low-fat—were measured out in bowls, waiting to be made into what he guessed was Athena's egg-white omelet recipe. A simple, filling meal from her first cookbook.

"You're critiquing our pretend cooking?" he asked, wondering how this was supposed to work.

"No, our on-camera chemistry and personality. Our *brand*." Athena lifted her hands in exasperation, looking as though she was about to cast a dark spell on the man with the sparse facial hair.

"Hello, Tina. Good to see you." Mullens gave her a warm smile that went unreturned unless an exasperated sigh counted. He grabbed the small black box from the counter and handed it to her.

"What's this?" Her eyes narrowed as she stroked the box's velvet exterior with her thumb.

"A hostess gift."

"Sorry? A what?"

"Open it."

She lifted the lid, revealing white-gold hockey stick earrings, each with a puck that held what he figured was her birthstone, an emerald. She looked up at him in confusion.

"It's hockey themed."

And, he was realizing, a bit much.

* * *

Athena stared at the half-inch-long gorgeous earrings. Gold. And were those real emeralds in the pucks? They were a casual design, dangly, with open hooks for sliding through her pierced earlobes, but they were obviously expensive.

Ridiculously so.

She closed the box. "Most people bring food."

"What kind of food do you bring a celebrated cookbook author? Also, it's Christmas tomorrow, so…" He shrugged.

"And so you're out of food?"

He gave her a chiding look, clearly unimpressed.

But being Greek, she did understand not arriving emptied-handed. Her family showed up with food. Pastries in particular. Maybe Chad couldn't spend time with a woman without having to bribe her with jewels. It probably helped them overlook his annoying personality.

"They're cute and themed," Nuvella stated. "Put them on."

Athena hesitated. The earrings were way too much. She couldn't accept them. This was a girlfriend gift. A bribe.

An apology?

She opened the box and took a second look.

Nope. Still gorgeous and ridiculous.

"Put them on," the woman repeated.

Athena sucked in a breath, tucked her growing-out bangs behind her ears and removed the small birthstone studs she'd received from her parents on her sixteenth birthday. She replaced them with the hockey sticks.

"Looks nice," Chad said.

"But no jersey," Athena snapped, plucking at his shirt. "This is an NHL thing, not specific to the Dragons."

"The Dragons are a part of the NHL," he argued.

"Take it off," she insisted.

"You want me to undress?" He grinned and began pulling at his jersey again, taking the tee he wore underneath along with it and revealing an expanse of tight abs.

Athena looked away, furious at the heat that crept into her cheeks.

"The jersey stays," Nuvella said. Her bleached hair was slicked back in an especially severe way today, matching her tone. "The recipes were created for Dragons players and on Dragons' time."

Before Athena could protest the inaccuracy of that fact, Chad dropped his jersey back into place and said, "So you're comping her costs for food and stuff? Sweet."

"What?" The head of PR frowned at him.

"Because this is a Dragons promo thing? So they should foot the bill, right?" He pulled his phone from his back pocket. "Let me ask Daisy-Mae. She's good about knowing the ins and outs of this stuff as she's always working on promos."

"No. No, it's fine. Athena will be compensated for her expenses," Nuvella said quickly, no doubt wanting to avoid being schooled by the team's ticket holder experience manager. Daisy-Mae might be new at her job, but she had a natural talent for bringing added fun to the home games, pulling the team into the limelight and creating loyal fans. This video series and the expense details might be beyond her field of expertise, but she was like the anti-venom for all things Nuvella. Daisy-Mae had been giving the PR pro a run for her money since the day she'd been hired—and even before then—and apparently Chad wasn't afraid to use her.

"Athena," Nuvella said tightly, "send in your receipts."

"Good." Chad put away his phone and Athena marveled at his smooth efficiency. She hated to admit it, but she could learn a few tricks from him.

"Also, aren't we making Athena's egg-white omelet?" He frowned at the ingredients as if there was something wrong with them. "That's from her first cookbook, which came out before she started with the Dragons."

Dang. This man should have been a lawyer or detective.

But wait… Athena surveyed the laid-out ingredients. How did he know what she was going to make, and the recipe's publishing history? Obviously, his agent had thoroughly prepped him.

"Well, the jersey stays," Nuvella stated with a sniff. "It identifies you as a celeb even to those who don't know sports."

"The Dragons aren't exactly a selling feature, given their losing streak," the man behind the camera muttered.

"We're a new team," Chad growled.

Howell cleared his throat and adjusted the camera's angle. "Stand closer."

"So my other NHL guests are going to wear their team jerseys as well?" Athena asked, frowning at Chad as he obeyed Howell's orders and stepped closer to her.

"I suppose," Nuvella stated reluctantly.

"Wait—I thought I was a regular on here?" Chad pulled out his phone again. "I need to talk to my agent."

"And roll," Howell said.

Chad sent a text message, then looked around as though expecting to be handed a script. "What am I supposed to do?"

"Look pretty while I work," Athena grumbled.

CHAPTER 4

"Hey," Mullens said quietly, after watching Athena toss ingredients around for a few minutes.

The camera guy was full of commands, including confusing ones such as not turning her back when she wanted to access the stove—which was behind her. How the man expected her to make an omelet was beyond Mullens.

"What do you want me to do?" he asked.

The glint in Athena's eyes suggested she wanted him to curl up and die, but she said with surprising lightness, "What I say. So, basically do whatever you want. I'm sure gold will rain down on you either way."

He choked on a laugh.

She caught him eyeing her earrings and she nervously fingered the left one. He could tell she'd been reluctant to accept the gift, and hadn't wanted to put them on. But she had.

This show meant a lot to her. Ditto for him. His career might even depend on it.

"We need to find our groove," he said. "Bring out your fiery side. Viewers will love it."

"I proposed a murder mystery theme," she replied, her tone sassy enough that he wasn't quite sure if she was kidding. She grabbed an opened bottle of red wine from beside a large pot, no doubt intended for a different recipe, and lifted it to her lips. After taking several long, slow gulps she set it down again and exhaled deeply.

What?

She gave him a challenging look. "Ready to find our groove?"

Her top lip was deliciously moist from the wine, and the mascara she was wearing made her pretty eyes stand out. This woman, whether she knew it or not, would always have the upper hand with him.

"Jersey on or off?" he whispered, aware of the hint of intimacy in his question.

"Jersey *on*," Nuvella snapped from the other side of the counter.

"What do *you* say?"

Earlier she'd looked as though she might go after him with that deadly blade lying beside the bowl of mushrooms. Now her gaze was warmer. It wouldn't thaw a steak or anything, but it wouldn't turn him into a popsicle, either.

"There's broccoli in the omelet I'm making." She wet her lips with her tongue, her brown eyes darting over the fabric covering his chest, then up to the tattoo that peeked out from the collar of his jersey. He resisted rubbing his fingers over it like a touchstone. It was a reminder of a life that had just begun, of a promise for the future and all the things he wanted.

"Broccoli?" he prompted.

"Now, I know you dislike broccoli, which really makes me wonder what you *do* eat...."

He froze. The joke. That stupid kid's joke about broccoli and boogers she'd told the group of players the day they'd met. It was the same one that used to have his sister, Evonne, in stitches of laughter.

Athena was going to tell the joke. In front of the camera.

He gripped the edge of the counter, promising himself that this time he'd hold it together. Not shut down or lash out at her.

Realizing his left hand had lifted to touch his family tree tattoo, including the small bird that was half angel flying above his collar, he sucked in an unsteady breath.

"Don't say it," he groaned, trying to make his pained tone sound like it was all about the stupid joke.

Athena turned to the camera, all brightness and sunshine. "What's the difference between boogers and broccoli?"

"That's it. I'm taking off my jersey." He did not need to hear that kids ate boogers, and hence, not broccoli. Not today. Not right now. Mullens started pulling off his shirt, taking his base-layer tee with it.

"Jersey on!" Nuvella snapped.

"Keep your clothes on," Athena muttered, her cheeks pink, her gaze locked on his exposed midriff. "This isn't that kind of video."

With false seriousness he pulled out his phone again as though he needed to make a call. "Then there's been a mistake. I have to talk to my agent."

Athena snorted and dropped a hand on her hip. "When you're ready, we're going to make an egg-white omelet."

"Speak to the camera," the man by the tripod commanded.

She sighed and turned back to the waiting camera.

"Oh, hey. What's your name again?" Mullens asked him. He reached across the counter, hand extended.

"Howell. Address the camera. Pretend I'm not here."

"Hard to do that when he's snapping at us," Mullens muttered to Athena as he straightened again. She rewarded him with a brief smile.

"To reduce cholesterol, we're going to make our omelet using egg whites." She began cracking eggs, that small smile playing at the corner of her lips. She deftly dropped the yolk from one half of the open shell into the other, letting the whites drain into the bowl below.

"We'll be editing the video, so don't worry about any lags or pauses," Howell said.

Beside Mullens, Athena tensed again.

Mullens wanted to shove the guy in a locker to shut him up, but there didn't seem to be one in the kitchen.

"Think he'd fit under the sink?" he whispered to Athena.

"We'd have to turn our backs to the camera," she muttered. Her eyes danced and the corners of her lips slipped upward before she caught herself.

"What do you do with the yolks?" Mullens asked. Each morning when he had his omelet he felt guilty tossing them out, to the point that some days he folded them back in again.

"Toss them."

"Seems wasteful."

"If you're baking, some recipes call for just yolks. You can plan ahead so you don't waste either of them."

Yolks probably meant a dessert. Something rich. What would be this woman's weakness?

"That probably outweighs the benefits of having an egg-white omelet for breakfast," he said.

"It does," she admitted.

Their eyes met and her smile turned slightly devilish.

Who was this woman?

"Ms. Gavras!" He placed his palms flat on the counter and gaped at her, pretending to be shocked. "You sneak brownies, don't you? Brownies rich in egg yolks!"

Her cheeks turned pink. "How do you know they're brownies?"

"Busted!" He turned to the camera and pressed his hands to his cheeks, unable to fully process the new truth, that Ms. Rules was, in fact, Ms. Rule-breaker.

Darned if his crush on her didn't just expand even further. All she needed was a pair of large-framed glasses balanced on her cute little nose and he'd be a complete goner.

"I'm not the pro athlete here." She pointed the shiny blade of a knife at him. "I can have brownies."

"I thought you were our role model."

"I'm not?"

He waited for the smirk. No smirk. Dang.

"Wait." He frowned at her, feeling as though he might have the beginning of a valid argument. "You told the team it's about moderation. Not denial."

She rolled her eyes and said drily, "Like you know anything about moderation."

He dropped an elbow onto the counter and leaned in, lowering his voice. "When it comes to something good... I don't believe in denial. Or moderation."

Athena deadpanned, "I'm confused. Are we talking about women or cars now?"

"We'll cut that." Howell said flatly. "Off brand."

"No, it's fun," Nuvella said. "Interesting."

Mullens tried to contain his laughter. Finally, he gave up, tipped his head back and let it out. Athena, warmed up by the joking or maybe the stolen swigs of wine, simply rolled her eyes and bit her bottom lip to stop what he was certain could have been a shared, slightly wicked smile.

* * *

Athena pushed a knife across the small space between them. "Can you chop the mushrooms, please?"

Mullens set to work, noting that she had stopped moving and was watching, her hands poised as if she wanted to jump in and take over.

Catching herself, she started whisking the egg whites.

"Howell? What do you think about Athena seeing a stylist?" Nuvella asked, her tone thoughtful. "The sweater is a pleasant color, but I'm thinking something sexier to really pull in the male viewers."

"She has nice curves," Howell agreed.

"That's sexual harassment," Mullens growled. "And she's already plenty sexy."

Athena's arm jerked, flicking the whisk and sending strings of egg whites onto the counter.

"Her publisher suggested something less bookish?" Howell said delicately, pressing a finger to his chin.

Athena touched her shiny locks and glanced down at her outfit. "What's so bookish about this?"

"Bookish is her brand," Mullens stated firmly. "She's written a bestselling cookbook. You're standing in... Is this your place?" he asked Athena. She nodded. "You're standing in her soon-to-be bookstore. Bookish *is* her brand. And she's smart. Ask her anything about food."

Howell protested, "I just want this to be—"

"Ask her."

The man sighed and waved a hand. "Fine. Carry on."

Mullens glared at him for an extra beat, then asked Athena, "Do you need to wash mushrooms?"

"What? Oh. You can dust the debris off their skin with a soft brush." Her tone was wary, her face red.

"But aren't they grown in…" Mullens looked at the camera. "Can we swear?"

"Definitely not. Start your conversation over from the top," Howell said.

"We're making a simple, delicious egg-white omelet today," Athena said, her voice rising with stress.

"No," Howell said in exasperation. "Talk about the mushrooms."

"Hey, how about you critique the video once we're done? And while you're gone…" Mullens moved around the counter, using his size to edge Howell toward the kitchen's back exit that led into the storage area and then out to the alley "…how about you Google how to deliver a compliment burger?"

"What's a—"

"Nuvella, you can go out there with him. He's going to need help with this."

The publicity manager scooted out the door like Mullens was chasing her.

"What's it called again?" Howell peered at his phone screen as he typed in a search query.

"It's a compliment, then constructive criticism, followed by another compliment. Compliments are the buns." Mullens pushed the man outside, where it had started to rain. "Athena's the real talent in this video series. Figure it out or don't come back."

"But my—"

"I said figure it out." He shut the door in the protesting man's face.

* * *

Athena hustled back to her spot behind the counter and tried to appear as though she hadn't been eavesdropping. Or swooning over the way Chad had shoved Howell from the building without even touching him.

Swoony.

Delicious.

And so off-limits.

And why was she swooning? The man was a hot mess. Who brought a "hostess gift" to a video shoot? And expensive jewelry at that?

He was trying to bribe her into forgiving him, even though he didn't deserve it.

She ought to return his gorgeous little earrings out of principle.

As Chad rounded the corner into the kitchen, she schooled her expression, set down her phone, where she'd been pretending to text her sister, and lifted her eyebrows. "I have a family supper in an hour."

He gave a curt nod, his expression dark, hinting at protectiveness or anger. She wasn't sure which. He glanced at the camera. "That thing still rolling?"

She shrugged and pulled at the neck of her sweater. It felt hot in here all of a sudden.

"All right," he announced. "From the top."

Suddenly he was all business, taking the cooking as seriously as his practices. Yeah, she'd watched a couple. It was her *job.* She needed to see what her players were doing on the ice so she'd know how best to fuel them. That was all.

"What's your deal?" she asked Chad.

"There is no deal."

There certainly was. He'd rammed his way into this project, was being charming but not smarmy, and then he'd defended her like she was someone important to him.

"Do you need to wash mushrooms?" Chad held up a handful. "Because I was told they grow in manure."

"Commercially grown mushrooms aren't," Athena said.

"We should introduce ourselves."

"Why? So you can finally get my name right?"

"To the camera. For the intro."

"Oh. Yeah, that's a good idea."

Chad dropped one elbow to the counter and grinned at the camera. "I'm Mullens, forward for the San Antonio Dragons. And today our gorgeous team dietitian is working me in the kitchen." He waggled his eyebrows.

"Seriously?"

"Flirty stuff sells. Smile to the camera."

"I don't flirt."

"Yeah." His face scrunched into a frown as he looked at her. "It would probably kill you."

"Hey!" She gave him a playful shove, immediately embarrassed for acting flirtatious.

Damn his charm and the fancy earrings. He *was* winning her over despite herself.

Chad turned back to the camera. "It's going to get hot in here, so stay tuned."

Athena sighed. "There's going to be so much editing to do," she muttered, then pasted on a smile.

"No, give us a real one," he said.

She widened it.

"No, not the sweet shark smile you get when you report a player to the coach."

Her smile disappeared. She didn't actually enjoy that. She'd much rather they'd follow her plans willingly, and get fitter and stronger.

"Fine." She turned to the camera, knowing her expression was slightly dark. Really, just a typical around-Chadwick kind of look. "I'm Athena Gavras, author of the cookbook *Eat Like a Player*." She held up a giant knife. "And today I'm not only going to show you how to make a quick, healthy breakfast, but also how to murder conceited players who think they're above following my dietary rules."

She gave Chad a fiendish grin, and he took an involuntary half step back. With rounded eyes, he stared at the camera.

"I'm going to stay right over here." He picked up the bowl of chopped spinach. "And eat my greens." He shoved a handful in his mouth, leaving most of it sticking out, like a horse eating grass.

Schooling her smirk, Athena slid the knife toward him, handle first. "But as a show of trust...how about you finish chopping the mushrooms."

"If I disappear," he stage-whispered to the camera, "check her alibi."

"Oh, I'll have a solid one, even though you'll be in the trunk of my car." She patted his broad shoulder. "But don't worry, I'll head up a search party to come looking for you." She gave him a syrupy smile. "Because I care."

He began slicing mushrooms. "Be sure to check her trunk first."

She nudged him away from the cutting board, then took the knife from his grip.

Chad cowered and raised his hands playfully. "Please don't murder me."

"The way you're murdering these poor mushrooms?" She shook her head, then swiftly removed the tough stem ends. "You'll need to forgive him," she said, demonstrating how to slice the mushrooms. "He knows his way around a *great* many things. Although the kitchen and my recipes and diet plans are not on that list. You can learn alongside him if you're a newbie, too."

She gave him a sweet, placating smile while continuing to chop, secretly enjoying herself much more than she could ever have anticipated.

* * *

"It'll be a miracle if they can turn that mess into a video worth sharing with the world." Athena jerked a thumb toward the kitchen, where they'd just finished filming.

Howell and Nuvella had left, having spent most of the remaining time in the alley.

Athena was acting almost friendly now, and had invited him to the front of her soon-to-be bookstore and café for a coffee. A Christmas miracle?

This part of the building was as much of a disaster zone as the back, but there was a shiny machine on the front counter, near where a cash register would likely go, and a promising hint of espresso in the air.

Athena's fuzzy sweater hugged her curves like a reverent lover while she worked levers on the coffee machine, and Mullens wondered if the fabric was as soft as it looked.

"Are you done?" A woman with untamed, wavy black hair

popped up from behind a stack of boxes near the front window.

Athena sucked in a breath and pressed a hand to her chest, and Mullens instinctively stepped between the two.

"Meddy!" Athena scolded. "You scared me."

"Sorry, I was sorting." She winced, stretching her lower back, hands on her hips. "I think I've done all I can. Any word on the shelves?"

"Myles said he'd come install them after Christmas."

"Good."

"You must be Athena's sister?" Mullens stepped forward, hand extended. "I'm Mullens."

She sealed her lips and she hummed a long, thoughtful "*hmm*" while looking him over. "I'm Meddy. Welcome to the future Huckleberry Bookshop." She crossed the distance to shake his hand, giving it one quick pump before she turned and slipped to the door, adding, "Catch y'all later! I'll be shooting darts with Dad at the Watering Hole if you need me."

Before the door had a chance to close, her head popped back through. "Don't forget—Mom and Dad's at five-thirty, and bring our cinnamon for the melomakarona. Dad forgot to get more."

Athena, quick as a baseball pitcher trying to strike out a batter, tossed a glass shaker of cinnamon to her sister. "Take it with you."

She caught it and frowned at the container. "I have to play darts with cinnamon in my pocket?"

"Do you want cookies later? Because you know I'll forget."

Meddy stuck out her tongue.

Mullens turned to Athena as her sister left, but she was already back to making the espresso machine steam and hiss.

"You were surprisingly comfortable in the kitchen," she said, glancing at him over her shoulder.

"Make sure that's decaf and sugar free," he teased, as she dropped an espresso shot into the latte she was making.

"It's better with sugar," she said absently. "And it's not like you follow the rules anyway, right?"

"Are you enabling me? No!" He gasped dramatically. "You're setting me up. You're framing me. Where's the camera?" He glanced around as though afraid he was being secretly recorded. "Are you live-streaming this to Louis?"

She shook her head, actually smiling at his jokes. Progress.

"It's about moderation, right?" Her usual tough, rule-follower persona appeared to be long gone. "Plus tomorrow is Christmas. The biggest dietary-rule-breaking day of the year."

"I thought you'd be into tea, not coffee."

"Who said I don't have a thing for tea? Huckleberry, blueberry, peach… Some teas are high in antioxidants, you know." She cast another glance over her shoulder.

"Who's this guy?" Mullens asked, noticing a gray tabby curled up in a basket set on top of some boxes. The cat's head seemed too big for its body, but judging from the overflowing dish of dry food on the floor, it wouldn't be long before the feline's skinny torso caught up with the size of its noggin.

"Clem. Brant says we bought his house, and that he has rights. Can't give him the boot—not that we would."

"The cat's name is Clem?" Mullens confirmed, rubbing its ears.

"Yeah."

The feline closed his amber eyes and smiled, leaning into Mullens' hand. "Who's Brant?" *Boyfriend? Landlord?*

"He's the local animal control officer and veterinarian." She gestured toward the back of the building. "There's a broken vent that leads to the alley that Clem uses as a cat door."

"Will you take him home once you open up shop?" Having a cat in a working café was surely a no-no.

She shrugged and passed a chipped white cup his way.

The drink smelled heavenly.

She took a sip of her own latte, her lashes fluttering as she enjoyed the hit of hot liquid. And then it was back to business with her watching him warily over the rim of her cup.

This would be a good time to confess that he didn't flaunt her rules nearly as much as he let everyone believe.

"Wait. I get the name. Clem as in Clemens?"

Athena nodded, a lock of hair falling forward and brushing her cheek. She quickly tucked it back behind her ear, but it escaped again.

"You named him?"

"Brant did."

"Clem," Mullens mumbled, petting the cat. Named after Samuel Clemens, the man who wrote *Huckleberry Finn* under the famous pen name of Mark Twain. "Clever." He said to the animal, " Suits you and your giant head."

Mullens took a sip of his latte and the sweetness hit his taste buds with a one-two knockout punch. His eyelids drifted shut. He missed sugar.

"Good, right?"

He opened his eyes to find Athena grinning at him.

Mullens set down his cup, feeling uncomfortable. He gestured to the mishmash surrounding them. Unassembled bookshelves, stacks of boxes and dishes.

"When do you open?"

"Next month."

He choked on an inhale. "And you're doing this while

publishing a cookbook and working for the Dragons?" He'd pegged her as an overachiever, but this was crazy. "Don't enjoy having free time, huh?"

She sipped her coffee, not answering, just glancing around the room as though adding things to her mental to-do list.

"I'm the same," he said. "What do you do when you're not working?"

"Open stores, obviously." She grinned, and he chuckled.

"Are those boxes in your office at the arena for here?"

"Hey, do you want that in a cup to-go? It's Christmas Eve." She checked her watch. "I'm sure you have places to be."

She was kicking him out? Already?

"Thanks." He handed her his cup. As tasty as it was, he'd seen how much sweetener had gone into it. Taking the drink with him would be a polite way to avoid finishing it, as well as the inevitable sugar crash later tonight.

Athena opened a box, pulling out a stack of paper cups. She grabbed his mug, poured the contents into the disposable one and handed it to him. "Sorry, I'm not sure where the lids are."

"You know, I can recommend a good business coach if you need one."

"We're going to run this ourselves," she said, gently herding him toward the shop's front door.

"No, not a manager. A coach. Basically, they help you prioritize, deal with overwhelm and mindset, as well as keep you focused on your vision."

Athena had been reaching for the door's lock, but lowered her hand, peering at him. "Do *you* have a business coach?"

"Of course."

Her eyes crinkled with amusement, her grin disbelieving.

She unlocked the door and gave it a yank to let him out onto the sidewalk in front of his parked car.

"No, really," he said. "How do you think I've leveraged my position in the NHL? Fame doesn't just happen. The commercials, product endorsements… This is a business, and my image has been carefully cultivated."

"So you're not actually a playboy?" She pointed at his beautiful Porsche from the doorway. "Rich man with fast cars?"

"Well," he said with a grin, "everything good should be based in truth."

The door closed on him, and he sighed, wondering if he'd ever figure out the key to unlocking Athena Gavras.

CHAPTER 5

"He should be here," Athena complained to Meddy as the makeup artist packed up her kit. They'd already shot the images of her for the cookbook's back cover and interior. It hadn't taken long, since Chad was supposed to be standing beside her in almost all of the planned shots.

The lights had been hot and the feeling of being stood up —or worse, pranked—had made her awkward and stiff. She figured this morning's photos would be toss-aways. Just like the food she'd prepped as props.

"Maybe he went somewhere fun for Christmas and his flight got canceled or delayed," Meddy suggested.

"He sent me his location—from here—two hours ago." They hadn't been able to find the photographer's building and Chad had sent her a pin. Meaning he'd been here.

But by the time they'd arrived—a healthy twenty minutes before she'd been told to—he was gone.

Stood up?

All he'd texted was "Got to take care of something. Back quick."

Then radio silence.

She sighed. She'd really wanted today off. Not just to deal with the post-Christmas sugar hangover from all the traditional Greek treats she'd baked—and then eaten—with her family, but because she needed a break.

But no. In marches Chad Mullens and suddenly everything ran on his schedule and she had to come in on her day off.

"Is it any surprise?" Her sister shrugged, her feet propped up on what was supposed to be Chad's beauty station, as she flipped through a book catalog.

Athena had promised Meddy they'd pick up some stuff for their store after the shoot and before Athena returned to her office for the afternoon. Technically, she had the entire day off, but since she was already in the city Meddy had suggested she take care of a few things at work so she could be stolen away later next week for some bookshop errands.

Athena smacked the booklet from her sister's grip. "We have more stock than we can sell in the first quarter. Don't tempt yourself."

"Hey! Don't take your frustrations out on me." She leaned forward and retrieved the glossy catalog.

The makeup artist hoisted her bags. "I'm leaving, but you're all set for when Mullens arrives." The woman with heavy eye shadow and a lip ring glanced toward the door as though reluctant to miss out on seeing the city's semi-famous hockey playboy.

"Did you happen to see him earlier?" Athena asked, before taking a sip of her lukewarm coffee.

The woman gave her a look, shoulders dropping as though

Athena had done something wrong. Athena followed her disapproving glance to the ring of lipstick she'd just left on her takeout cup. She winced apologetically. "Sorry."

"I didn't see him, and I was here early." The artist set down a bag, fished out a lipstick and tossed it over. "Keep it. And here are some disposable makeup wipes. When you're done, you can use them to clean your face."

"Thanks."

The artist left and Athena muttered, "The man needs to buy a watch."

"When do you want to have our first open-mic poetry night?" Meddy asked. "I was thinking soon after we open the store. Maybe the second week? Get people in the habit of checking us out."

She nodded absently. "Sure. But I don't understand him. I mean, he was great at the filming. He ran Howell and Nuvella off the set so I could relax, and even defended my sexiness."

"He what?" Meddy turned abruptly, feet back on the floor, brows furrowed in curiosity.

Athena got that excited, breathy feeling just thinking about the way he'd defended her and her nerdy bookworm side. He'd even called her smart—that had earned him extra brownie points. Brownie points he was currently scarfing down.

"He brought me earrings, and he—"

"The gold hockey sticks?" Her sister's lips turned up in a devilish grin. "He's got a crush on you."

"Obviously not." She frowned at her watch, not willing to admit that she'd toyed with the ludicrous idea a time or two before telling herself to get a life. "He's just trying to win me over so he doesn't get in more trouble with the team's management."

"Hmm." Her sister sat back again, catalog open but her hazel eyes on Athena.

"I don't get it. He knew the omelet recipe was from my first cookbook. But he doesn't cook. He disregards everything I say or do or—"

"Yeesh. Take a chill pill already. No wonder he's ghosting you." Meddy tossed the catalog onto the small makeup counter in front of her. "Don't forget there's a reason you quit hockey players. Let him go. Move on."

Athena grumbled to herself, pulled out her phone and texted her friend Jenny Oliver.

Know any single professors? I need a date.

"What are you doing?" Meddy asked.

"Looking for a bookworm to date."

"Mullens is making you feel things, huh?" That evil grin was back.

"Primarily rage."

Jenny texted back, *I'll ask Karen.*

Smart. Ask the local librarian.

Athena checked her watch yet again. Chad was so late. They were supposed to be done by now. "He is such a self-centered man."

"He's also hot and going to sell a crap-ton of your cookbooks."

"I know." She sighed. "But he's just like Lonnie. All promises and charm, but can't keep a commitment."

Her sister rolled her eyes. She'd made no bones about letting Athena know how she felt about Lonnie when she'd started dating the man. Their parents had been quieter about it, but she'd noticed he didn't get many dinner invitations after the first one, and his first family game night at the Gavrases had been his last.

"He's a player."

"You're smitten, but you hate it, don't you?" Meddy's eyes narrowed as she studied her older sister. "He's making you feel all tingly inside, but insecure because you think he'd never choose you. And if he did, you fear he'd treat you like crap, just as Lonnie did."

Athena glared at her. "Have you been reading the psychology section instead of putting those books on the shelves? We have to discount them if you crack the spines, you know."

Her sister just grinned, as if she'd broken the code explaining Athena's bad mood.

Darn her family, always seeing right through everything. Why couldn't she suppress her crush-like feelings and move on without anybody noticing what a loser she was for lusting after the so-totally-wrong guy?

"I don't think he's as big of a player as he pretends to be. And anyway, it's a bit early in the day for Mullens to be waylaid by women or drink." Her sister stood, slinging her large, beaded purse over her shoulder.

"It's never too early."

"Have you ever been wined, dined and wooed on a Friday morning?"

Her mood darkened. "No." But now she kind of wanted to be.

"Let's ditch."

"What if he shows?"

"Give lover-boy a taste of his own tardy medicine and leave. Don't be the pathetic woman who puts her own life on hold, sitting around ready and waiting until he deigns to show up."

"Nobody says 'tardy' anymore."

Her sister smirked. "Come on, I want to go poke at some credit card readers for the store. You promised you'd help me decide."

Athena held up a finger. "Just gimme another minute."

She dialed Chad. No answer. She texted him, waiting to see if he'd shoot back a reply. Nothing.

Not cool.

* * *

With her face freshly scrubbed of most of the photo-session makeup, Athena stood in the San Antonio sunshine, fuming that she'd been right about Chad. He was cut from the same cloth as Lonnie. He would never fully respect her or her time.

Meddy stood on the passenger side of Athena's car, waiting for her door to be unlocked.

"Just a sec."

"Do. Not. Call him," her sister commanded.

"I'm not." She tapped her phone, realizing Chad still had his location shared with her from earlier. He was five blocks away at a convention center and hotel.

Gotcha.

"I have to do something." She tossed Meddy her keys.

"Athena!"

"I know. I'm sorry. It's already too late to go, anyway. I don't have time to cross town and also get ahead on my work. Take my car and pick whichever card reader you want."

Her sister's eyes narrowed, her shoulder-length earrings swinging. "Where ya going?"

"Someone needs a piece of my mind."

"Promise me you won't give him so many pieces it makes you stupid."

"Meddy!"

Her sister smirked, circling to the driver's side. "Oh, I almost forgot. I want to hire a contractor."

"But we already got our bookshelves sorted out."

"No, for Mom. An early Mother's Day gift."

"Mother's Day isn't for five months."

"I know. But she can't get onto the porch in her wheelchair without help, and Dad needs freedom. She needs independence, and sitting on the porch is good for her. It's less isolating."

Athena nodded, realizing how true that was. Their mom used to read, knit and sip sweet tea on the covered porch, and call out to neighbors as they went by. In many ways, that was her social life.

"A little plywood and some nails, and boom! Some ramps so she can come and go on her own. Dad would do it, but he'd probably nail himself to something."

Athena laughed softly. Their dad was a lot of things, but not handy. "Okay. I'm in. I'll cover half."

Meddy grinned and took off in Athena's car, tooting the horn as she pulled away from the curb.

Athena, holding on to her frustration with Chad, stormed across the city's downtown, formulating what she wanted to say. Who did he think he was? Elbowing his way into her project and then ditching so he could go have a quickie?

She was supposed to be shopping with her sister, not tracking him down.

A few minutes later, with her doubts pushing aside her anger, Athena stood outside the conference center. She checked her phone for his location. Still inside.

She smoothed her shirt over her middle and entered the building, pausing in the grand lobby. Sparkling chandelier, black stone shiny underfoot, tall plants and cozy sitting areas with leather chairs… Voices and laughter drifted in from several conference rooms.

Would he get a room under his own name or an alias?

She headed toward the check-in desk, tentatively circling past a few open meeting room doors to buy herself some thinking time. A sign on a tripod said SPCSN: Sunshine: Parents of Children with Special Needs. Various sessions were listed below in smaller font.

Long tables stretched across the room to her right, with an aisle down the middle that led to the lectern. In a second room, a cluster of people were seated near the center.

She continued past, then slowed her steps, processing what she'd seen.

Wide shoulders. Longish black hair that touched the edge of his Dragons jersey.

Dragons jersey?

Chadwick?

She stopped. *No.*

There was no way.

She tried to keep going, but found herself taking several steps backward so she could peer through the doorway again.

His deep voice reached her. Too low for her to make out the words, but she understood the soothing tone.

She stepped inside without thinking.

As though feeling her gaze on him, Chad looked up, dropping the hand that had been rubbing the back of a tearful woman in her fifties. Others in the room followed his attention, and soon a dozen sets of eyes were on her. Some were wet or rimmed with red, and a box of tissues rested on one of the tables.

"Sorry," Athena said uncertainly. Everything she'd planned to say to Chad fled, along with her anger.

No, she was still angry. If he was speaking at a conference or whatever it was, he could have let her know.

But he wasn't speaking, was he?

What was this? Did he have a child? She'd sensed something out of sync with his playboy persona. Was it fatherhood?

Maybe everything she'd assumed about him was wrong. Maybe he was the father of a special-needs child and she'd just walked in on his big secret.

But the most worrisome idea whirling through her head was that maybe—just maybe—her crush wasn't that out of place after all.

* * *

By the time Mullens caught up with Athena she was in her arena office, slamming her hand down on a hole punch, her brow furrowed.

He watched from the doorway as she yanked the papers out, ripping a few in the process. She let out a cute growl, then took a new sheaf of papers and shoved them into the device. Before she could destroy that batch, he slipped into the room and gently laid a hand over hers. He took the stack, culled it down to half before completing the job and neatly setting the papers on her desk.

"Sorry I missed the shoot," he said quietly, taking a step back.

She planted her right hand on her hip and tipped her head, looking at him with those dark eyes. The stage makeup they'd put on her was for the most part wiped away, but her lashes were still thick and long, creating big-eyed pools that gutted him.

"Why?" she asked, her tone just as careful as his own.

"What?" He'd been expecting a fight and her calmness left him off balance. "Because it's important to you."

"No. Why did you skip out? I know you were there before our shoot time. I missed shopping for card readers with my sister because I stuck around waiting for you. Why'd you leave before I arrived?"

"Oh." He rubbed his eyes and exhaled, suddenly exhausted. "I messed up my schedule. Right place, wrong time."

Whenever he dealt with something connected to his late sister, Evonne, he got a little fuzzy in the head and messed stuff up. He felt like he was a scared, lost kid all over again.

He hated it.

And he certainly wasn't going to talk about it with Athena.

"You were supposed to be at a conference before the shoot?" she asked.

He nodded once. "Quick photo op."

"For what?"

"Just handing over a check. A post-Christmas, year-end gift." He smiled as if the donation was all about getting a bit of tax relief from Uncle Sam. "Hey, so I'm wondering if we can reschedule the photographers and ask them to come here. Save you some time and hassle."

"That wasn't a photo op I walked in on at the conference center."

"I got to talking," he said, not willing to get into how he knew those kind, hurting people. He gave what he hoped was his usual cavalier grin. "You know how it is, being famous."

"No, I don't, actually."

"Well, you soon will! We're going to take this cookbook to

the moon for you." He edged toward the door. "And since I know you're busy, and I let you down, I'll get it all sorted out, okay?"

"Chad?"

He paused, hovering on the threshold. So close to safety. "Hmm?"

"Are you a dad?"

* * *

Athena parked her car—which had somehow magically filled itself with boxes of books from her office—and hustled to the building that held the Dragons' head offices. Her mind was a swirling mess, as it had been for the past several days—ever since she'd found Chad being cried on at the conference for parents of special-needs children.

Who on earth was Chadwick Mullens? Who was he *really*?

He'd laughed at her when she'd asked if he was a father. *Laughed.*

She'd been softening toward him, believing that if he was the dad of such a child, it could explain that sensitive side he studiously hid from the world. And maybe even explain that hint of lost little boy she sometimes saw flickering in his light brown eyes.

But she'd been duped. He wasn't a dad, and he'd left her office clearly amused.

The man was hiding something. But if not a child, then what?

She wanted to box him up, write him off and move on. But the intriguing, infuriating unknowns that kept popping up were driving her crazy. What if he *was* a nice guy and she was dismissing him for all the wrong reasons?

Then again, what man hid who he really was from the world or those who knew him?

And why would she even want to spend time around someone who didn't show her respect in the workplace?

Because he was hot, mysterious, and had stood up for her with Nuvella and Howell?

Yeah, that was a lame set of reasons.

She grumbled to herself and hoped her meeting with Nuvella and Daisy-Mae Ray would go well. If the two women weren't on the same page as she was about promoting her new cookbook, it was going to turn into a big mess. It had all been so much easier before Chad had gotten involved. Just her and a few NHL mucky-mucks.

As she neared the building, she lifted her oversized sunglasses. A familiar, wide-shouldered man was at the base of the concrete steps.

Chad Mullens.

How was he everywhere—except at important photo shoots? Which still hadn't been rescheduled because of his apparently fully booked calendar.

Athena drew closer, rolling her eyes. Was he signing something for the man in the wheelchair? As if Chad needed his ego padded any further.

No. There was no autographing happening. They were gesturing to the left, where a crew was resurfacing the wheelchair ramp, and Athena tensed. Inaccessible buildings were a hot button now that her mother often relied on a wheelchair when a lot of walking was involved in her outings.

Before Athena could reach the duo, Chad flagged down a man in a suit, gesturing where to grab the chair on the opposite side.

"Tina, hold his briefcase, would you?" he commanded.

Before she could think or react, she was holding the black leather case, and Chad and the stranger were lifting the chair, passenger and all, straight up the steps.

Athena followed slowly, admiring Chad's problem-solving skills and compassion. The two men set down the wheelchair and passenger, and Chad pushed the automatic door opener, gesturing for Athena to follow the man inside.

Dang it. She was going to have to rethink her frustration and anger with Chad once again, wasn't she?

"Hey, Tina."

Nope. Maybe not.

He was still as irritating as an anthill under a picnic blanket. His agent had obviously coached him to perform enough good deeds that the public didn't hate or resent him. "You keeping that briefcase, Tina?"

Realizing she was hugging the stranger's case, she jerked, then thrust it at the amused man. Ignoring Chad, she pivoted and beelined across the lobby, her cheeks burning in embarrassment.

While she waited for the elevator, she heard Chad's deep voice as he spoke to the security guard posted a few feet inside the doors. "Can you let him out the back exit after his meeting? The front ramp's out of commission."

The elevator doors opened and Athena walked in, surprisingly disappointed that Chad wouldn't be riding up with her. She jabbed the button for Nuvella's floor.

The security guard's voice carried across the tiled entry. "We don't let people in, but we always let them out."

Male laughter filtered toward her.

Just before the elevator closed, an arm reached out, causing the doors to jerk open again. Chad squeezed his way in. "Hey. Going up?"

"Only direction possible." She pushed the Open button. "Is your friend coming?"

"Who?"

She gestured to the lobby, where the man he'd helped was still joking with the security guard.

"He'll catch the next one." Chad reached across her and hit Close. "Got a meeting? Or do you have an office in here, too?"

"Meeting."

"Me, too."

"With Nuvella?" she asked, facing him, dread and hope battling it out in her chest.

"Miranda." The team's owner.

Athena smiled, hoping it was that sharkish one he feared. "So today you get fired?"

He scoffed. "Never. I'm also meeting with Dak."

Miranda's boyfriend, who ran the team's sick kids' charity. Interesting.

She hated to admit it, but all Chad had to do was tenderly hold a kitten and her ovaries would probably claim they had descended from seahorses and, like seahorses, mated for life, and he was their chosen one. Good thing it was too early in the year for a litter of kittens to be dropped into his lap.

"Another photo op?" she asked, filling the silence.

"Nope."

"Wait…" She felt a wicked grin spread across her face. "The big bad playboy is going to donate all of his fancy cars to the Dragons' charity?"

He laughed. "Not a chance."

"Not even one?"

He tipped his head as though considering it, then gave a small shake.

"How many do you have?"

"Three."

"Three cars for one little man?"

His brows lowered and his shoulders seemed to expand several inches with his next intake of breath. "I can hardly call myself little. And yes. Three."

"Why?"

"In case one breaks down."

She waited for him to laugh, to admit that he reveled in the status of owning three luxury cars. Or maybe he enjoyed throwing his money around, or needed the cars to match his top three moods or outfit vibes, or some such thing.

But no. That was his answer, and gazing at him, she understood that it was the actual, real reason.

She was tempted to tease him about what might be a misplaced fear of abandonment—by his vehicle on the side of the road with nobody who loved him enough to come rescue him—but resisted. Partly because she understood that helpless feeling of a vehicle letting you down.

The doors opened on the wrong floor and he hit the Close button again.

"So you're going to go hang out with sick kids?" she asked, referring to his meeting with Miranda and Dak.

Some of the players had been doing hospital visits, brightening the days of ill children as part of the team's charity. After seeing Chad help the stranger in the wheelchair, as well as talking with the parents of special-needs children at the conference center, him being involved didn't seem like such a crazy idea.

"Not today." He clasped his hands in front of him as he watched the floors light up on the panel above as they began to move again.

"Monetary donations?" she asked, feeling as though her

gentle ribbing to pass the time had become more of a burning curiosity.

"Do they need money?" He swiveled to face her, his expression serious.

She sensed that if she named a sum he'd donate that amount to the charity. She shrugged. "Probably."

He was watching her out the side of his eyes. His gaze traced from her bare toes peeking out of the bottom of her black stovepipe pants to her white silk, sleeveless blouse with the high neck and open back. Then up to the ballerina bun she'd wrangled her hair in, leaving several curly tendrils to frame her jaw.

"You're wearing your earrings wrong."

Her fingers flew to the hockey sticks. How could you wear earrings wrong?

And why did he have to catch her wearing them? She knew she should have buried them in the bottom of her sock drawer so she could forget all about them and never give him the satisfaction of knowing she actually liked them.

"Here." He shifted so he was standing in front of her, her back to the elevator wall. When his large hands reached for her face she tensed, thinking for a moment that he was going to kiss her.

He huffed out a laugh. "Relax, Tina." He gently plucked the earrings from her ears, palming the jewelry.

For a big burly hockey player, he was surprisingly tender.

He took one of the earrings, and with a gentle and, strangely erotic tug, slid the hook into place before repeating his actions on the opposite side. His gaze slipped to hers, his moves leisurely.

"Much better."

The elevator doors opened, but neither of them budged.

"The hockey sticks should face inward."

"Oh."

The doors closed. The elevator moved downward again.

"They were expensive, weren't they?" she asked, immediately wishing she hadn't.

"I have a deal," he said automatically. She wasn't certain if he truly had some sort of bulk discount with a jeweler—he might, given the number of women who normally hung around him. But she got the feeling he was actually masking something.

His warm palms had settled on her shoulders. She watched his Adam's apple bob as he slid his hands upward until they were cupping her head, his thumbs caressing her jaw.

She held her breath as his body pressed against hers.

Her eyelids drifted lower.

The doors dinged open again, and sounds from the lobby filled the elevator. Chad blinked, stepping backward.

He cleared his throat, then got out on the wrong floor.

CHAPTER 6

"How's it taste?" Mullens asked, leaning against the counter in the bookshop's kitchen. It was just the two of them and the camera on an early Saturday morning, having graduated from Nuvella and Howell's school of film making.

Athena had teased him like they were friends earlier in the week when they'd ridden the elevator together. She'd maybe even flirted a bit, revealing that playful side he'd seen her expose only when she thought he wasn't around.

He'd been unable to sleep or focus since that ride. His thoughts had been stuck, wondering what might have happened if the elevator doors hadn't opened.

Would he have kissed her? Would she have let him?

That would have been a miracle—as big as her seeming to have forgiven him for the whole photo shoot mishap. Then again, maybe he'd just caught her in a moment in that elevator, because today she was hyper-focused, her mind clearly not on him.

He missed fun Athena and wanted her to come out and play.

For the camera.

Ha. Who was he kidding? He wanted all of Athena, and preferably in his arms.

"The walnuts?" he prompted, when she didn't answer his earlier question.

Athena, concentrating more than he figured was necessary on slicing a fresh pear, grabbed one of the still-warm, lightly candied walnut halves from the dish and held it out. She was in the zone, forgetting about the camera.

It was clear she expected him to put out his palm for it. Instead, he crouched slightly, lining his mouth up with her fingers. Time to make some magic happen.

She jerked in surprise when his warm breath danced across her knuckles. As she flinched, his mouth closed, nipping at her fingers.

"Did you just bite me?" Her dark brown eyes went wide.

"And usually women have to ask," he replied, waggling his eyebrows.

"How did I get so lucky?" She shook out her hand as though trying to flick away pain. His teeth had barely grazed her, but he knew that wasn't what she was recovering from.

He was messing with her mind.

Athena focused on her pears again, braising them for the arugula salad. She talked to the camera, informing their future viewers about cooking temperatures, what sort of flavors went together, and how to be brave in the kitchen without ruining the entire meal.

"Let me taste." He was at her elbow, leaning over her dish of pears.

She tipped the bowl toward the camera as if she'd been

cooking for an audience all her life. "You'll notice they're perfect. Bits of golden edges. Not mushy. Firm in all the right ways."

"Like me."

"Like you," she said absently, spearing a pear with a fork. She held it out. "Careful. It's hot."

"So are you."

Her face turned a cute pink. "It'll burn your mouth."

"Let me… blow on it." He smiled devilishly.

She sighed and knocked the pear off the fork onto a waiting plate, refusing to play with him. "Try it with some dressing." She whisked the homemade blend, stirring up the various ingredients again before dripping some on the pear. "Drizzle it on top like so…."

He gave the cooked fruit a dubious glance. It didn't look as gorgeous with the dressing on top.

Athena scooped up the piece with her fingers and took a tentative bite, holding her other hand under her jaw to catch any drips. "Mmm. That's tasty."

"You lie."

"I do not. Try it."

He tipped his chin in her direction, coming close enough he could practically steal a bite from her.

"Get your own."

"No." His mouth darted out, encompassing the pear as well as her fingers.

"Hey!" She tried to jerk her hand away, but he clasped her wrist, holding it in place while he swallowed the fruit, then lazily licked her fingers.

Oh, that was good. That was stirring some things deep down inside, and with her, too, judging from her dazed expression.

His eyes locked on hers and she glared at him without conviction, her voice breathy when she said, "Can you not behave for more than one second?"

"Where's the fun in that?"

He watched as she battled with herself about how much to enjoy, how much to let go. A familiar old argument.

This time he hoped she lost.

* * *

"Anyone here?" called a voice.

Athena popped up from where she'd been munching on her pear and arugula salad with Chad in the kitchen, studiously avoiding looking at him.

"In here, Jenny!"

Thank goodness her friend was dropping by. Athena had texted her sister to come watch them film under the pretence of wanting feedback, but actually afraid that if she spent much time alone with Chad they'd be filming a sex tape rather than a cooking show.

But Meddy had declined, with a lame excuse that she had to pay the contractor who'd done a few odd jobs on the store. Hadn't she heard of sending an e-transfer? She could do that from this very kitchen while supervising the filming.

Athena didn't know why Chad was getting under her skin so badly today. Probably because he was making her want things, and he was all wrong for her.

And his aftershave? How did it smell more tantalizing every time she saw him? She understood why the women in his commercials swooned so convincingly after he patted it on. Those actresses had stolen that paycheck. She'd bet they hadn't had to "act" even one bit.

"I'm in here!" she called again, weaving her way into the back room, to find Jenny holding a box and peering into the dimness.

Athena hit the lights as her friend explained, "I signed for this yesterday."

"Meddy, ugh!" Athena took the package and checked the shipping label. "She keeps using this address even though we're not around enough to receive everything. Thanks for catching this for us."

"No problem. How's the store coming along?"

"Slow. Chad and I are filming videos for the cookbook's channel today." Next week she'd be working with a different player, thank goodness. It had been decided that Chad would feature in every other show, giving her a much needed reprieve to collect herself and inform her ovaries about the reality of genetics—that they weren't related to seahorses and would accept whomever *she* chose.

"I should get out of your hair," Jenny said.

"Hey! It's Dylan's girl," Chad said from the kitchen doorway.

She turned bright red. "Uh. No, we're not—"

"He talks about you."

"Oh, well. Um."

"Dylan O'Neill? From the Dragons?" Athena asked, staring at Jenny. She'd heard all about how the two had bickered and butted heads at Thanksgiving. She'd figured they'd burned that potential relationship bridge, then bulldozed the surrounding land for good measure.

"Maybe I'm mistaken." Chad came closer, bringing the delicious scents of candied fruit and his aftershave with him. "I'm Mullens."

"Right. I'm Jenny Oliver."

"So you're not seeing anyone?" Chad asked. They shook hands, and pink splotches appeared on Jenny's cheeks when he held hers a beat too long. His smile was kind and so sincere that Athena wanted to throttle him for being such an incurable flirt.

"Oh, uh, not really."

"What do you look for in a man?"

"Chadwick, leave her alone."

Wait. Was she feeling jealous of Jenny or protective? It *was* protectiveness, right? It had to be. Because jealousy would be the height of stupidity and Athena had promised herself she'd left stupid behind when she'd packed up and left Lonnie.

But she couldn't help noticing that her friend, who was normally pretty feisty around the opposite sex, seemed a bit awed by Chad.

Yeah, she got it. He had this way of turning women into gooey puddles—*all* women. So fight it, girl. The man was *such* a player.

"Seriously, Chad, boundaries," Athena scolded. "Not every woman wants to be another conquest. Do you not have a sister? What if Jenny is someone's sister? Would you want some playboy macking on her?"

Chad's expression went blank, his mouth a stony line. Athena sighed. Seriously, of all the things she rode him about, he was going to get butt-hurt over his very public flirtatious reputation?

"Come on," she said, battling her rising guilt over his sudden drop in mood. "You have a new woman on your arm in every photo."

"I'm not dating them," he said moodily.

"Exactly!"

"Or...that."

"You're not sleeping with them? Just snapping pics for social media?" She'd heard that one before.

"That's right," he said, his tone suggesting she was dense to have assumed otherwise.

She rolled her eyes and turned to Jenny.

"Speaking of seeing someone," her friend said, her starry-eyed Chadwick spell broken. "Karen got you a date."

"What? She did?" Athena clapped a hand over her mouth and stilled her dancing feet. "I totally forgot I'd asked! Is he a professor type?"

"He's an *actual* professor!"

"No. Way. January is totally looking up!" A date with a bookworm would be the perfect distraction from this silly thing she had going on between herself and Chad. Not that she likely even registered on his sliding scale of women. "What's he a professor of?"

"Literature, I think."

Athena grinned.

"Perfect, right?" Jenny said.

She nodded, already dreaming about a home library with two cozy armchairs, a fireplace and shelves filled with books.

"You don't have time to date," Chad said, his tone stern.

Athena glared at him. "Excuse me?"

"You have the shop, the cooking channel and your job as a dietician. You can't leave us all hanging."

"Who says I would?"

"Well, this looks like a good time for me to scoot," Jenny said. "I'll get Karen to text you his number."

"Thanks." Athena turned to Chad, murder pulsing through her veins.

He raised his hands in surrender.

"No, no way." She pursued him as he backed into the

kitchen. "You don't tell me what to do, and then shut down the conversation when I call you on it."

"You're needed by the team."

"You don't even have appointments with me anymore."

"Uh..." His eyes cut left, then right. "Louis put me back on your roster—"

"He *what?*" Athena pulled up short, realizing she was actually kind of happy about that. The coach had imposed a cease-fire and now neither of them had to lose face if they wanted to call a truce.

"My point is that my schedule is about to get *insane,* and so is yours when you open this shop in three weeks. When are you going to have time for a new relationship?"

Ugh. He was right.

"You know what, Chadwick?"

He pressed his right hand to his chest as though he was trying to calm his heart rate. Or maybe protect himself from the oncoming onslaught.

"You suck. A lot. And you know what else?"

"Hmm?"

She studied him, noting again the way he seemed afraid to meet her eyes. For all his bluster, swagger and confidence he was actually a vulnerable little boy sometimes, wasn't he?

She narrowed her eyes, trying to sort out what she saw. "You're not the big bad playboy you pretend to be. And I'm going to figure out who you really are."

* * *

Mullens watched Athena move about the kitchen as they filmed their second video of the day. The idea was to stockpile footage, have someone edit it, then schedule it all to go live on her channel closer to the cookbook's release date.

Or maybe she just wanted to get all the videos involving him done and over with so she could return to ignoring and despising him.

Which might not be such a bad idea if she truly was intent on unearthing his secrets. Part of him wouldn't mind having a woman share his life—the real stuff—but another part of him wanted nobody anywhere near the pain he'd buried long ago. That would be a sure way to send a woman running. Even a sweetheart like Athena.

She was working on the second recipe of the day, her moves confident, her energy high. This was her happy place. Maybe even more so now that she'd secured a date with a man who was Mullens' opposite.

Although she'd let him flirt with her in the first video.

Nibbles. Crossing the line and sucking on her fingers.

The thought made him grin like he'd achieved a lifetime goal.

Athena was tasty.

And she'd felt it, too. That sexual connection between them. The tension. The attraction.

Not that she seemed eager to give in to those feelings. She wanted a boring old professor with a high falutin' mind, not a millionaire who crashed into other jocks out on the ice.

He should back off. Forget her. Let her go.

Mullens wasn't anything like what she wanted, from the way he behaved on down to not having a close or loving family. Athena was literally starting a business with her sister and always texting or calling her parents, whereas he no longer had a sibling, and his parents were long done with him.

It was just him and his fancy cars, and anyone who cared to spend a little time with him.

And yet here he was, looking for an opening to flirt with Athena as if it might lead to them becoming something special to each other.

"Toss in about a tablespoon of oil. Like this," Athena said, gracefully dropping a dollop of olive oil into a heated wok.

"Why not coconut oil?" Mullens asked, pulling himself back to the here and now. He pushed aside the cooked chicken he'd cubed. "That would taste good with the sweet potato, wouldn't it?"

She gave him a surprised look.

Crap. He was supposed to be playing up the role she knew —the clueless man who didn't know the difference between arugula and iceberg lettuce. The guy who thought "the kitchen" was a trendy new bar.

"The smoke point of coconut oil isn't high enough for the heat we're using."

"Your coconuts are smokin'," he said, dropping his voice to a suggestive register.

"Someone save me," she muttered under her breath, tossing the vegetables into the wok.

"I know mouth-to-mouth." He leaned close, aware he was within striking distance.

Athena looked up from her task, her eyes lingering on his lips.

"Imagining what that might be like, Tina?"

"Actually, imagining how many lips have touched yours." Hers curled in the most adorable way as she went back to abusing the food over high heat, breaking down fibers or some such thing.

His few conquests suddenly felt like less of a badge of honor than they once had.

By the time they were done cooking their stir-fry, Mullens was sweating from keeping up with Athena. He wasn't bad at food prep, but he wasn't a ninja like she was. He had a feeling she enjoyed keeping him hopping, asking for ingredients he was still working on.

Coach could learn a few tricks from this woman when it came to getting a player to hustle.

"Man, is it just me, or is it hot in here?" He wiped his brow with the hem of his shirt, not caring if he was showing the world his abs and breaking food prep rules, or whatever Athena would surely find to scold him over.

"It's just you." She gave him a sly smile that stunned him.

He literally didn't know what to say, so turned to the camera and stared blankly at it. Out of the corner of his eye he spotted Athena's shoulders shaking as though she was holding in a laugh.

"You been into the cooking wine again?" he asked.

"Never." Her expression suddenly grew serious, and he looked around to find the steady, assessing gaze of her sister locked on them.

He checked his watch. Yup. Just about time for Athena to move on to her next job—whipping this building into shape. Wait, no. Tonight was a family dinner, bringing back memories of his own family, when his sister was still with them. She'd been a great fan of pancakes, and as a surprise he'd made her a huge feast one night. It ended up being their last meal with her.

She'd been thrilled, her hands moving a mile a minute as she used sign language between bites, telling him what an awesome brother he was and how much she loved him.

Carrot cake pancakes with whipped cream, sliced bananas and lots of blueberry syrup. They'd laughed, eaten, and then the next day it had all fallen apart, her being raced to the hospital with a pain in her gut that had been serious enough to take her life. Their parents had never said what it was exactly, just that her body, as fickle as it had always been, had simply given up its fight against one of her many underlying conditions.

They'd told him it hadn't been the pancake feast. That it was just poor timing.

But Mullens could only believe that they were trying to spare his feelings.

Meddy was looking at her watch, chewing on her lower lip and jiggling her leg as though she was running late. Athena kept a tighter schedule than Mullens did, and it made him wonder what she was hiding from. Did she keep busy as a tactic to avoid thinking about or feeling something?

A sliver of guilt rippled through his mind that maybe she was avoiding thinking about *him* and how his attitude encouraged the team to give her a rough time.

If he could go back to the day they'd met in that meeting room, he'd change it all. He would simply walk out and collect himself instead of trying to hold it in. He would be mature and not snap at her over the carrot-and-walnut pancake recipe.

Mullens let out a long, slow breath and shoved his fingers through his hair, trying to ground himself in the here, the now.

Forget the past. Forget the pain. Channel himself in this moment.

Athena waved a forkful of root vegetable stir-fry in front of him. "Try it."

"What's with the fork?"

"You prefer chopsticks?" She huffed a laugh when she realized what he meant. "You think I'm a slow learner? There'll always be a utensil between that mouth and my body from now on."

"Aw," he said, trying to play up his faked disappointment. "That's no fun."

"Exactly."

"You don't enjoy fun?"

"No, I do. It just looks different than your version."

"So you don't love hanging out and feeling good with someone?" His body was close enough to brush against hers. She was turning a delightful pink, but stood her ground. Maybe she was afraid to step outside the camera's view and wreck the footage. Or maybe she liked it right where she was.

"Is that how you define your love life?" she asked. "Hanging out and feeling good with someone?"

He lowered his mouth, taking the forkful of stir-fry. Unsurprisingly, it was delicious.

"You've never dated a hockey player before, huh?"

There was a bright flash in her eyes. "Who says I haven't?"

Was that a challenge? No. It was something else. Truth?

Truth and pain.

His breath caught just above his sternum as his thoughts collided. "Who was he?"

"I don't kiss and tell."

"Lonnie," Athena's sister interjected from her spot just offstage, glancing up from her cell phone.

"Meddy!"

"What? He would have just pulled out his phone and looked it up online."

"Online?" Mullens asked. Lonnie. Hockey player named Lonnie… No. Absolutely not. There was no way.

That crazy forward from New Jersey?

Mullens heard a gasp, realizing it was coming from himself. His whole body felt like it had been lit up from the inside as the truth blossomed, stealing his breath away.

"You've dated hockey players!" He slapped his hands on the counter, then turned to the camera. "Guys! *Guys!* She dates *hockey players!*"

Forget boring, stuffy old professors. She needed someone fun. Maybe a professional athlete. Someone who'd make her light up and laugh. He wasn't saying a professor couldn't do that for her, but he was pretty sure that her looking to date one was simply a knee-jerk reaction from dating Lonnie. Heck, Mullens would probably go that route himself after a go-around with that yahoo.

He sidled closer to Athena, so close she could barely work without elbowing him. Actually, she did elbow him. Possibly on purpose. But it lacked her usual conviction.

"Wanna go out with me?" he asked, lowering his voice in a way one of his exes had described as sexalicious. "You don't have to cook, and I'll only bite if you ask nicely."

Her face had gone bright red, and she clamped her jaw at an odd angle like she was fighting the urge to scream.

"What? Is that a yes? No? I'll think about it?"

"She's having an aneurism," Meddy said with amusement.

Athena simply shook her head and added liquid coconut oil and chilli powder to the vegetables. She left the wok on high heat for less than a minute, tossing the contents, then pouring them out into a serving dish.

"Can I try?"

She snatched a clean fork from the stainless steel counter-top, scooped up a mouthful of steaming veggies and held it out for him to take. She waved it impatiently when he didn't respond. The food smelled wonderful, but he knew what would make better footage.

He shook his head like a stubborn toddler, crossing his arms. "Only if you make choo-choo sounds."

She gave a dramatic, full-bodied sigh. "Aren't you a big boy? Can't you feed yourself?"

"No." He angled closer, keeping his mouth closed. It was either this or grab her around the waist and pull her in, and he was pretty sure she wasn't game for that.

Plus he didn't especially want to create footage where she was kneeing him in the family jewels. That would surely go viral when the guy working in the editing room thought it would make a funny outtake.

Meddy giggled from behind the camera, and Athena shook her head in exasperation. "Choo, choo!" her sister said encouragingly.

With a dramatic sigh, Athena said in a voice one might use with a baby, "Open up, here comes the veggie train. Choo-choo!"

Mullens couldn't believe he'd gotten her to do that. In front of the camera, no less. She really was a different person in the kitchen.

Obediently, he opened his mouth, and she dropped in the food. His taste buds exploded with a burst of flavors.

"How does that taste better than when I make it?" he asked in wonder, his mouth still full. At one time his mom would have murdered him for such poor manners. Now he wasn't even sure if she'd bother to tune in to the show.

Athena laughed, then stopped abruptly, studying him.

Uh-oh.

"More?" he asked hopefully.

CHAPTER 7

"What is he doing?" Athena leaned across the diner's red-and-white-checkered tablecloth to look past her date, Glenn, a professor of literature.

She lowered her hands, realizing she'd been waving them about in indignation.

The man at the other table was an adult. He could do what he wanted.

Even if it was a direct attempt to get a rise out of her.

Glenn turned to peer over his shoulder at Chad Mullens, and Athena grabbed his wrist, startling him. "Don't look."

But she couldn't resist doing so. He was wearing a body-hugging black sweater and jeans, and was manspreading at his table for one, his shoulders practically as wide as the table itself, greasy food piled up in front of him. Then again, Athena figured, a built hockey player such as Chad couldn't help but manspread. His quads were so stacked with muscle he probably couldn't sit with his legs together even if he'd wanted to. She'd seen him in the gym, seen the girth of those bare thighs shoving weights the size of a small car up a metal incline.

Okay, not quite *that* big. But big enough.

"I forgot. Karen says you're a dietician?" Glenn glanced around the small-town diner, then winced at his almost empty plate. The poor man was clearly afraid she was going to lecture him about the saturated fat content of his burger and fries.

"I'm sorry. I promise I won't rant and rave about your meal. You can eat whatever you want."

He smiled politely as Chad took an enormous bite of his own cheeseburger, juice dripping off his hand and onto his plate.

"Um. Can you excuse me a moment?" Athena slid from her chair.

She shook her head as she moved past Chad, studiously avoiding looking at him. Just like she had since he'd walked in —right after she'd sat down with her date. What was Chad even doing in town? They were done filming until April.

Athena pushed open the bathroom door and whipped out her phone to text her sister. *Chad is here.*

She chewed her lip and waited for Meddy to reply. She was across the street shelving new books and listening to music on her phone. Or she had been when Athena had left her there forty-five minutes ago. Why wasn't she answering?

"Are you okay?" Jenny asked breathlessly, the bathroom door banging shut behind her. Her cheeks were rosy from being out in the early January chill.

"What?" Athena blinked at her.

She pointed toward the front of the diner on the other side of the wall. "I was walking back to the store—" her clothing shop, Blue Tumbleweed, was right next door "—and saw you and your date."

"Glenn."

"Glenn. Then you hustled away like you were going to be sick. Are you okay?"

"What? Yes." Athena leaned forward, her indignation rising again. "Did you *see* him out there?"

"Glenn?" Her friend tried for a smile. "He's older than I expected and he seems to have a passion for brown clothing, but he's nice, right?" Her tone became tentative.

"No, Chad."

"Who?"

"Chadwick *Mullens*."

"Oh, yeah. Mullens. I said hi to him on my way by. Henry's watching him eat like it's his favorite game show."

"What?" Why would Henry Wylder, a man who was grumpy about everything and everyone, be focused on Chad? Whatever the reason was, it couldn't be a good one.

Jenny shrugged. "He actually seemed entertained. He almost *smiled*." She gave Athena a meaningful look.

"It's all worse than I thought." Henry didn't smile about anything. Ever. If even he was succumbing to the Chadwick Mullens charm effect, then what hope did Athena have as a mere mortal woman?

Her phone vibrated with an incoming text. Meddy. *I thought you were going out with the teacher guy. Nice score on getting Mullens instead!*

Athena let out a frustrated growl and tapped out a quick reply. *Not with him!!! Fill you in later. Jenny's here.*

She put her phone away and focused on her friend.

"So, you have a date with both men?"

"No!" She frowned at Jenny. "Ew."

"Okay, so you're dating Mullens? But he found out you're seeing Glenn on the side?"

"What? No! Ugh. Why does everyone think I'd go out with

Chad? That man is not getting anywhere near me for a date. And why is he even here? Why's he in town, sitting at that table thumbing his nose at me?"

"Free country?" Jenny was watching her carefully, as though Athena was becoming unglued.

Maybe she was.

During the last filming she could have sworn Chad was familiar with her cookbook and recipes. He'd blown off the few comments he'd made about cooking as though he'd been faking culinary knowledge for the cameras. But it had initiated enough doubt that Athena no longer felt she could believe anything about the man.

She clasped a hand to her forehead, collecting her thoughts. "He ordered onion rings and a milkshake."

"Oh, I love Mrs. Fisher's milkshakes."

"I know. Me, too. But they're *forbidden*."

"Oh, right. The hockey player diet thing." Jenny lowered her voice. "Do you think he's trying to ruin your date?"

"What? Why?"

"I don't know." Her tone was innocent, but a small, satisfied smile was playing on her lips.

"What? Tell me."

"He likes you."

"He likes anyone with two X chromosomes."

Jenny chuckled. "And you don't want a hockey player, am I right?"

"Heartbreakers."

"I see." She glanced down, then up again. "All of them?"

Athena shrugged. "He's just… I've seen him on TV. Always signing something for a chick and they're always hanging off of him. They wouldn't do that if he wasn't welcoming."

"How does he act in real life?"

Athena rolled her eyes. "Total flirt."

"Fun though?"

"He's awful."

"Why?"

"I like him even though I shouldn't." She crossed her arms, baffled as to why she was so into him when she should be giving him a wide berth. "And he doesn't take me seriously at work."

"Maybe because you take yourself *too* seriously?"

"I'm in my thirties. I have a birthday coming up. I'm supposed to *be* serious."

Jenny waved her hand again. "But he makes you laugh."

"Sometimes, yeah."

"So then, who says you have to give him your heart? Can't you just crush on the man and let that be it?"

"What do you mean?"

"Has he asked you out?"

"No."

"There you go."

Now she felt insulted that he hadn't asked her on a date. Well, at least in a way that felt real. Like he had stakes in her answer.

"You can find a guy sexy and have fun with him without dating him," Jenny said. "There's this new-fangled thing called being friends. It even works between opposite genders."

"Ha-ha," Athena replied flatly.

"For real. You've been driving yourself so hard lately with all this work. Let the guy make you laugh. Let loose a little and have some fun."

* * *

"So you're a professor," Athena said gamely, sliding back into her spot across from Glenn.

Have fun. Let loose. Laugh a little.

And don't take Chad so darn seriously.

Jenny, who'd waited for Athena to leave the washroom first, moved past Chad's table, stealing an onion ring from his plate.

"Hey, I'm telling Dylan you're a thief!" he protested.

"He already knows." She leaned forward, mocking. "I stole that grumpy bear's heart, didn't I?"

"Really?" Chad gave her a reassessing look. "I thought you two hated each other?"

Jenny laughed, waving him off. "Mullens, you can't steal what doesn't exist!"

She walked past Athena, surreptitiously giving her two thumbs up.

Athena smiled but kept her focus on Glenn. Not Chadwick Mullens, who was breaking every nutrition rule a smart pro athlete would religiously follow.

The man was like a toddler begging for attention.

"We've both published books," Glenn said, smiling at her. Their plates had been cleared away even though she hadn't quite finished, and Athena wondered if their date was winding down.

She took a sip of her herbal tea, grateful it hadn't been taken away as well. "Oh?"

"Karen said you've put together a cookbook?"

"Yes. I'm working on a second one right now and we're donating a lot of the proceeds to charity." Thanks to Chad.

She hated to admit how much his gesture had warmed her heart. Any thoughts of sabotaging his involvement in her project had gone straight out the window when her agent had mentioned that part.

"You cook?"

"I do."

"I don't." He smiled like he'd struck gold.

Her attention drifted to Chad again, and she thought back to several remarks he'd made while cooking. Despite his image, the man knew his way around a kitchen.

She eyed his sweater and how it stretched over his tight shoulders, his rock-hard abs. That man didn't eat onion rings. Not regularly.

Or stacks of doughnuts, which had arrived while she'd been in the washroom. Same with the slice of chocolate-coconut pie.

How could one human even eat all that, after his double cheeseburger with bacon, fries and onion rings?

She sighed, wishing she could ban Mrs. Fisher from delivering any more food to the Dragons' star forward.

"No wonder the team can't bag a *W*," she muttered.

"A what?"

Athena blinked at Glenn, realizing her attention had drifted again. "Oh! Sorry. Sports speak. It means a win. The Dragons are one of the worst-ranked teams in the league."

"I don't follow football."

"It's, uh, hockey."

He laughed good-naturedly, his kind face bright and open.

"Better not admit to the football thing around here," she said out of the side of her mouth. She gestured to the TV in a back corner, which was playing college ball. Now that one of their own had made it to that level, the town was fully in when it came to the sport.

Glenn laughed again. "Thanks for the tip."

She smiled complacently. Sure, Glenn wasn't what you'd traditionally call hot, but he was easy to hang around.

Chad waved to Mrs. Fisher. "Mrs. F., can I get a soda? And make sure it's none of that diet stuff. I want sugar."

Athena locked her jaw, steeling herself. If he wanted to skate like his legs weighed eight hundred pounds in tomorrow's game, then fine. It was his choice. His career.

"I'm sure he can burn it off," Glenn said politely, noticing that her attention had drifted once again.

"The amount of fat, sugar, salt..." Athena closed her eyes.

Pieces of the Chad puzzle were swirling in her mind, driving her crazy.

He knew his way around a kitchen. Sure, his chopping skills needed help, and he didn't understand the smoke points of different cooking oils, but did the average person?

The truth, as she saw it, was that the man either cooked a fair amount, despite his protestations that he didn't, or else he put in significant time studying up before they filmed. Even though he couldn't possibly know what she was about to prepare and which skills he'd need.

But the biggest truth was that to get a body like his, he couldn't eat the way he was tonight.

In fact, he was looking paler than he had ten minutes ago, and he seemed to be losing speed the further he got into his binge-fest.

"He's messing with me," Athena muttered, dropping her elbows onto the table. "As always." She shook her head. Whatever Chad was up to, she would not let him ruin her date. "Hey, so you must like reading?"

Glenn lit up. "I do. Although mostly for work. Americanism and identity in novels published between 1855 and 1900 have been my siren's call lately."

"Interesting." She took a sip of her huckleberry tea, nodding politely.

There went the chance of sharing books in that cozy little home library she'd envisioned when she'd first heard about their potential date. Last night she'd stayed up way too late, having gotten sucked into a book she'd ordered for the store.

Just before Christmas she'd been joking with her friends Hannah and Cass about cavemen romance being a genre. One thing had led to another and suddenly she was up until two in the morning, chewing on the corner of her thumbnail as Corg went alpha on Lucy, claiming her in ways Athena didn't even realize existed.

Well, Chad probably did…

Speaking of the man, his usual healthy complexion seemed to have taken on a greenish tinge. Or was that just the diner's fluorescent lighting and her hopeful feelings related to his general doom?

Chad leaned back in his chair, his eyes scrunched shut, his face pale.

Good. She hoped he barfed in that beautiful red sports car he'd parked out front.

He stood suddenly, wavered on his feet and then beelined to the door, his complexion definitely an unnatural shade of green. He hit the door at top speed, and Athena gripped the edge of her table, thoughts tumbling through her mind.

It could be the flu.

Yes, it was probably the flu.

It definitely couldn't be an indicator that, when it came to his daily diet and what foods his body was used to, Chadwick Raul Mullens was a big, fat, sexy liar.

* * *

What had he been trying to prove? He was like a desperate teenager begging for attention, determined to come off as someone cool. He hadn't acted like this over a woman in, well, ever. Even as a teen he'd been too smart to act this dumb. Or at least too busy raising himself and working hard at hockey.

Mullens dropped his hands to his hips and paced the empty sidewalk outside the diner, glad to feel the roiling in his gut start to settle.

At least he hadn't barfed in the Longhorn Diner or out here on Main Street for all the town to see. The only problem was that now he had to go back in, pay his bill and walk past what was surely a gloating Athena—twice.

It could be worse, he thought, staring at his beautiful, cherry-red Corvette. He could have thrown up all over its pretty interior.

An older man with almost-white hair came sauntering out of the diner. He was a cowboy through and through, a frown deeply etched into the lines of his face. He spotted Mullens and came over to slap him on the shoulder.

"You sure can put that food away. I ain't seen nothin' like that since Carmichael was a teen. Oh, how our mother would get all up in arms. He'd eat everything in sight, like my great-nephew Myles. Only more!"

"Uh, thanks."

"No. Thank *you*." The man shook his hand, while placing his other one on Mullens' shoulder. He walked away, saying, "Good memories. Good memories."

Mullens straightened his spine and tipped his head back with a sigh. At least he'd impressed someone. The town was growing on him, and he'd been around often enough lately that a few faces were becoming familiar. Almost as if this place could become home if he spent more time here.

Determined to maintain what little pride he had left, he vowed to walk back inside without looking at Athena or her date, pay his bill and leave. He opened the door, ignoring the protestations coming from his gut as the scents of garlic, butter and grease hit his nostrils. Immediately someone's hands pressed against his chest. He glanced down in surprise, expecting Mrs. Fisher. The waitress probably thought he'd been trying to dine and dash. Except for the part about returning to the scene of the crime.

"It's taken care of. Head home," Athena said quietly, gently pushing him out onto the sidewalk. He backed up and she followed, crossing her arms against the chill in the evening air. She looked pretty, her hair tumbling to her shoulders, her clingy wool dress wrapping around her body like a lover, her tall dark leather boots hiding what he knew were gorgeous calves.

She was watching him, her eyes darting across his face, looking for clues—probably as to the reason for his asinine behavior.

"What do I owe you?" he asked.

She shook her head, a knowing smile softening her features.

"What?" He sucked in a breath and gritted his teeth as the scent of onion rings and fries wafted onto the street.

"Go home." She patted his arm, and he let his eyelids flutter closed.

"No, what do I owe you?" he pressed, knowing she'd understand he meant more than for just the meal.

"Are you all right to drive? Or are you too ill from all that heavy, heavy grease weighing like a rock in your stomach?"

His gut churned again as a rogue wave of indigestion hit him starboard side. "You're mean."

"As previously established," she said perkily. "And I learned it from you."

"Your date..." He gestured to the man who'd just left the diner. Dressed head to foot in dark beige, including shoes, pants, jacket and even a jaunty corduroy hat, it was like he'd stepped out of a sepia photo from the 1800s.

Athena turned, squeezing the man's elbow. "So lovely to have met you, Glenn."

He handed over her purse and jacket while Mullens propped himself up against his car. He'd deal with any scratches he made to the paint later. The two murmured something he couldn't hear, then her date left in a sedan that rattled with a loose muffler.

Mullens noted the lack of a goodbye kiss. The professor hadn't even tried.

He would have. Always go for the kiss. Especially with a woman like Athena.

She marched back toward Mullens, wetting her lips. After eyeing him carefully, she spun away again, her boots clipping along the sidewalk. "Hang tight," she called over her shoulder, before disappearing through a doorway that wasn't the diner's.

Curious, he drifted after her, stopping outside a small drugstore to wait. An armadillo waddled out from a narrow space between two buildings and Mullens froze, letting the animal do its thing. But instead of ignoring him, it came closer, sniffing his right foot before looking up at him with dark beady eyes, then ambling off again.

Athena returned moments later, waving a tube of chewable antacids, she tossed them at his chest. He caught them. Mint.

"I just met an armadillo."

"Bill? Ornery little critter? Gray? About yay high?" She bent down and held her hand about a foot off the ground. "Probably tried to eat your leg off?"

"Nah. Just sniffed my foot and wandered away." Mullens unrolled a few antacids. "You were fast. Did you even pay for these?"

"Couldn't have been Bill the armadillo then. Can you get yourself home?"

"Of course."

She was frowning down the street, where the armadillo was scurrying after a woman. The tall gal in the cowboy hat let out a squeal and jumped into a hardware store at the end of the block. Athena turned back to him, her brow furrowed.

"What?"

"Do you need a barf bucket?"

"I'm fine." He straightened, realizing he'd been hunching in discomfort. He chewed and swallowed the minty antacids, feeling they might be the all-important one-thing-too-many of the many, many things he'd eaten tonight. All of it getting chummy down in no-man's-land. A fresh wave of nausea was building inside him and he fought against it.

Athena was smirking, clearly very amused by his stupidity.

"You're laughing at me." He offered her the package, but she shook her head. "You think I'm an idiot."

"This…" she drew an air circle around her face, making no effort to hide her amusement "…is actually admiration."

If he'd been feeling up to it, his pride would be smarting.

Wait. Did she say admiration? For him acting like a total

jerk, disrespecting her knowledge and advice, as well as probably prematurely ending her date?

"What are you talking about, Tina?"

* * *

"You cling to this identity through thick and thin." Athena paused a second to school her expression. "And barf."

Jenny was right. She needed to laugh more. And laughing at Chad, especially when watching him bolt from the diner, had flipped a switch. Turned him from unattainable jock with a gigantic dietary chip on his shoulder to just some guy trying to look cool in front of others.

His flaunting her rules wasn't personal. It never had been. And now it was all oddly amusing.

"I didn't vomit." Chad leaned against his Corvette again, clearly disgusted with himself.

"The fact that you're so invested in this cool-dude, rule-breaking persona that you're willing to ralph your guts out on Main Street in front of everyone..." She shook her head, holding back a laugh.

"I didn't." He pushed himself off the hood, looking ready to argue.

"You take care of your body," she pointed out, tapping one of his sculpted shoulders, "even though you think it's uncool."

"I don't think that, but thanks for noticing..." He flexed his right biceps. "And anyway, you've always known I work out. Religiously."

She narrowed her eyes, tilting her head to the side. "Don't change the subject."

"I see you, Tina."

She made an unintelligible sound before blustering, "I don't know what you mean."

He gently touched her chin, drawing her face toward his. "You go by the arena's gym a *lot*." His fingers danced through her hair, his touch almost reverent. He stroked his hand through her hair, pulling a few strands as his fingers tangled.

"Ow!" She tried to pull her head away, protesting, until he held up a bobby pin that had been holding back her growing-out bangs. "My office is near the gym and I have recipes to deliver to lockers!"

Chad gave her a slightly scolding look, then smiled. A smile that seemed to suck the air from her universe, create black holes and supernovas of longing. His voice was low, rumbling in a way most women would consider alluring and incredibly sexy. "Don't worry, the feeling is mutual, babe."

"Conceited much?"

"Come on. You're hot." He was close, so close her breath hitched as the warmth from his body intensified her own. His fingers brushed through her hair again, sweeping it away from her face. He still had the bobby pin, and he deftly slid it into place, tying back the piece that usually fell across her face. "That dress you wore to the gala? Very sexy. And your clingy pink sweater?" He shook his head slowly, biting his lower lip.

She swallowed hard and tried to recall what they'd been talking about before he'd deftly changed the subject and washed her brain of all thought other than what it might feel like to straddle those strong, thick quads of his.

"Why do you fight me?" she asked, edging out of his force field. "You work out, but you crumple up my recipes and encourage the others to ignore me."

Those flirtatious eyes grew pained when her voice trembled. Athena shifted so she was resting against the car, her shoulder to his, facing forward so she didn't have to see the changes in his expression.

"It's not personal," Chad muttered, with a darkness to his tone that surprised her. Secrets, secrets, secrets.

"So then?" she prompted.

"This body doesn't just happen." He gestured to his chiseled, muscled form.

"You don't eat as much crap as you pretend to." Honestly, she should have clued in sooner. She'd been so preoccupied with the minutia she'd missed the big picture. "I'm onto you."

One corner of his mouth turned up devilishly. "You want to be on me like ham on cheese." But there was a lack of conviction in his flirtatious tone and, beside her, he inhaled deeply.

She leaned away to better take him in. Pale. Sweaty. Clearly unwell. "My word, you've wrecked yourself."

"Nope," he said, carefully rotating his shoulders. "I'm fine."

"Yeah?"

"Totally."

"So you don't need to barf? Want to ralph? Feel the need to hurl? Upchuck? Vomit?"

He hunched over, hands on his knees, inhaling slowly, methodically. Through gritted teeth, he said, "Everyone else is wrong about you. You're not just mean, you're cruel."

She laughed and slipped a hand into the crook of his elbow, her chest pressed against his arm. "Let me take you home," she said gently, resting her chin on his wide shoulder. The poor man was in no shape to drive himself all the way to the city.

"Yeah." He hoisted himself up and handed her the fob to his car.

"Why did you binge all of that?"

He didn't reply.

"To get my attention?" Her tone was soft. "Because it worked. You've got me here. Ruined my date and everything."

He groaned, running a hand through his dark hair. "I'd like to say I'm sorry, but he's the wrong guy."

"Yeah? How do you know?" She was more curious than upset. Probably because it had been clear within the first minute or two of meeting Glenn that they weren't a good match. Friends, maybe. But a love connection? Not quite.

"You need more thrills."

"Tried it. Didn't enjoy how it all panned out in the end."

Chad frowned as he moved to the passenger side. "Lonnie's not the right kind of guy. Neither is Professor Loves-Beige. You need a man who straddles the line somewhere between the two."

He wasn't wrong. She'd swung from one end of the spectrum to the other.

Athena gestured toward the diner. "Want me to grab a bucket or something?"

He shook his head.

"You sure?"

"I'm not puking in front of you. Or in my car."

"By sheer willpower alone," she announced in a deep, dramatic tone as she unlocked his gorgeous machine. He really must not be feeling well if he was letting her get behind the wheel of this sensational beast.

She opened the driver-side door, and the scent of Chad's dreamy aftershave wafted over her. It was going to be a long drive to the city.

"You need more laughs," Chad said.

"That's what Meddy and Jenny say."

"They're right."

"Yeah?" She was realizing that with each passing year she was becoming less fun. Without even noticing, she'd been carving it out of her life, bit by bit.

Maybe it really was time to let go a little and see where serendipity took her.

"And where can I find more laughs, Chad?"

"Start with me." He smiled at her over the Corvette's roof. "You laugh at me all the time."

CHAPTER 8

"Turn around." Mullens leaned across the console between himself and Athena, who was pressing down hard on the gas pedal of his zippy little sports car as they hit the outer limits of Sweetheart Creek, the expanse of highway opening up in front of them.

"No way. You said I could drive."

"It doesn't make sense for you to chauffeur me all the way home."

Athena gave a playful pout. "You just don't want me driving your beautiful baby." She dropped her chin and batted her eyelashes in a flirtatious way that had his heart gasping in shock. "I thought you were supposed to be fun."

Hello, sweetheart.

No, he reminded himself. This was Athena.

She might be flirting, but she'd turn as quickly as a spooked mare if he wasn't careful. He needed to be nothing like that dunce who'd almost barfed, trying to get her attention back there.

Then again, she was driving him home, which meant being stupid might finally give him a chance.

Although he was currently trying to convince her not to take care of him tonight. That, too, was stupid.

This woman got him so twisted up he couldn't even think straight. Her driving his Corvette was brilliant, and gave them time together. And tomorrow she'd need to return the car, and see him again. It was perfect, really.

"How are you going to get home if you drive me all the way back to San Antonio?" he asked, unable to help himself.

"You have three cars, don't you?" She looked gorgeous wearing that wide smile.

Yeah, there was no way he was going to do anything to pull that grin off her face.

"If you stay the night, I can drive you home in the morning."

She laughed. She might be relaxing around him, showing her playful side, but he knew she would never step across that self-imposed line and do something that crazy. At least not with him.

"So, besides letting you drive my car," he asked, "how else can I help you have more fun?"

"Actually—" she cut a quick glance in his direction "—watching you destroy yourself kind of made my day."

Mullens ran the heels of his hands down his quads and arched his back. The antacids and time were helping to settle his stomach, but he didn't exactly need reminders. Especially since his pride was in the process of catching up with him and his stupidity.

"It shouldn't matter to me whether or not you follow my dietary advice," she said, her tone perfectly level, "but it means a lot that you do."

She cut him another glance, this one assessing. Approving, even?

"Yeah, I'm sorry we got off on the wrong foot."

She snorted. "Understatement."

He could tell that his behavior confused her, and that she didn't quite trust him. He needed to show he was trustworthy, even if not entirely worthy of her forgiveness.

"Hey, why don't we go out on a date?" he asked, shifting in the passenger seat before she could ask him why he'd been such a jerk the day they'd met.

She kept her focus steady on the spool of straight highway unwinding in front of them.

"Tina?"

Her head began shaking back and forth.

"What? It would be fun." He dropped his voice. "And I bring delightful gifts."

He studied her earlobes. She was back to wearing the tiny emeralds he assumed were her birthstone.

"I am sure you'd be fun, but your lack of respect at work isn't exactly something I look for in a potential boyfriend."

"Right." He contemplated how to fix that, while his brain roared the word *boyfriend* in his ears. "I'm sorry about that."

"Sorry isn't enough."

"I know," he said in a low voice. "I do follow your diet, though."

"You cook?" She glanced over at him, her eyes unreadable.

"Yeah."

"So being cool is more important than showing me respect?"

"No, and the way I've treated you is unforgivable and awful," he admitted, feeling about as big as an ant.

She sighed. "Yeah."

They rode in silence for a few minutes. Finally, she said, "We want different things."

"Why? What do you want?"

She shrugged, a shadow crossing her face.

"Love?" he suggested.

"You don't?" Her tone hinted at disapproval. "No, you probably want action and adventure. Something short-lived."

"I really do have an excellent business manager, don't I?" He tried for a smile and she rolled her eyes.

"Fine. Change the subject, Mr. Cool."

"I wasn't. He does a good job of making sure that the image I put out there is the one that sticks."

"What does that mean?"

"I wouldn't say no to love."

She gave him an assessing glance before turning off the highway and onto another. "Marriage?"

"You proposing?"

"Well, apparently you got me pregnant with just one look, so you'd better make an honest woman of me."

He gasped. "Tina! Are you flirting with me?"

She laughed, a rich sound filling the car. "If I am, what are you going to do about it?"

He wasn't sure, but he had some ideas. "Okay, so you won't date me. Yet."

"I never said no."

Hope rose like waters during a flash flood. "Do you wanna go out with me? Supper tomorrow night?"

"No, thanks."

"Seriously?" He threw his hands in the air, knocking his ringed fingers against the side window. "You make me go through all of that just to turn me down?"

"Actually, I was thinking about what you said the other day." She pushed a strand of hair from her eyes.

Oh boy. What had he said now?

"I've taken on a lot lately. I basically have three jobs and I'm crazy busy—like you. It's a bad time to start a relationship. I might let someone down, you know? Leave them hanging."

He grumbled to himself. Her argument against dating him was the same one he'd used against her going out with Glenn.

"Fine. How about this? We are now officially friends." His tone was firm, and he hoped she wouldn't fight him.

She paused for an uncomfortable length of time. Probably only a second, but long enough for his heart to drop. "I guess."

He pressed on, despite her lack of enthusiasm. "And because you're busier than a sparrow making its spring nest—"

"I'm not nesting," she said hotly.

"—I'll surprise you one night by bringing you supper at the store."

"That sounds an awful lot like a date."

"Friends do nice things for each other," he explained. "I'll bring enough for your sister. So technically, it's just us being friends."

She narrowed her eyes. "You want to have supper with my sister?"

"She's part of the Tina package. Besides, I love how she gives you a hard time."

"She can be such a little brat."

He nodded, suddenly missing his own sister. The jokes. The endless agony of being a sibling, but also the unparalleled joy of having someone who'd always forgive you, always take your side when it mattered.

"Fine," he said, after clearing his throat. "We'll excuse her, and you'll squeeze out a half-hour break with me."

"So, you're making it a date?"

"I don't care what you call it or if we're eating on top of boxes of books or sitting on the floor," he declared. He hoped his take-charge tone wouldn't make her dig in even further. "You need a break, and so we're doing this. It's for your own good."

She was fighting a smile, clearly charmed.

Truthfully, he didn't really want to sit on the floor eating out of take-out containers. But if that's what it took to get Athena on a semblance of a date with him, so he could prove he was in fact a gentleman, then he was all in.

* * *

Athena hovered in the doorway of Chad's penthouse, having turned down the offer of a drink when she'd dropped him off. She *had* asked to use his washroom, though, curious to see his home.

She'd imagined dark, masculine colors and showy décor lacking in personality or homey touches. A man cave built around the blatant masculinity he projected. Basically, an architectural version of Chad's fancy cars and alpha reputation.

"You coming in?" he asked, his usually healthy glow having pretty much returned during the drive.

She crossed the threshold, clinging to the purse strap hanging over her shoulder as she looked around. Beneath her feet was a well-worn area rug covering polished black stone streaked with white. The entry was huge, bigger than her own apartment's living room.

Chad's penthouse, a jutting square at the top of a downtown building, had twelve-foot-high ceilings, giving it a very grand feel. From where she stood she could see through to the living room, airy and spacious and overlooking the city. Streetlights, building lights and cars below winked at her through tall windows as the January evening settled in.

This apartment in the sky, from what she could tell, had a million and one upgrades, and screamed *money*. And yet as she glanced around, she noticed the personal touches and gentle wear that made it a real home.

"Powder room's there," Chad said, pointing toward a door to her right.

She held back a smirk at hearing a man so large and in charge, covered in rings and a big tattoo, calling the bathroom by such a dainty name.

Covering part of the wall outside the bathroom were framed candid shots. Beneath, a long table was covered in a jumble of unopened mail and shipping boxes, gum wrappers and car keys.

She took in the photos, her gaze dancing over them before settling on one. There was a much younger Chad, a handsome boy without the rings or tattoos, but clearly him. His arm was around a girl in an electric wheelchair and they were grinning at the camera with that same perfect row of front teeth. Happiness.

"Who's this?" she asked, pointing to the photo.

Chad, who'd been hanging his jacket in an enormous entryway closet, turned her way. His face became expressionless, locking her out just like he had on that first day in the dietary clinic. He turned back to the closet, carefully shutting the doors. "My sister."

"I didn't know you had a sister."

"I did."

"Oh." She looked back at the photo, noting the joy, the closeness.

Did.

This young girl was gone.

Athena glanced back at Chad, but the stiffness in his shoulders made it clear he was done talking. "I'll be in the kitchen."

She shut herself in the powder room, wondering what had happened to his sister. She thought of Meddy and how devastating it would be to lose her.

Chad's sister in a wheelchair.

Her own mother in hers.

Did she and Chad have more in common than she'd realized?

The photo shoot he had been at for parents of children with special needs had to be related to his sister somehow. The man was a never-ending mystery, a tired soul who locked everything in instead of wearing it on his sleeve.

She flushed the toilet, reading the sign above it. *Go ahead, make yourself comfortable. No, not that comfortable. Keep your clothes on. Don't make things awkward.*

A bubble of laughter broke free before she could contain it. She could have guessed that Chad would be all about encouraging people to take their clothes off in his apartment. Especially the fairer sex.

As she stood at the sink, she looked up, taking a moment to realize the small, opaque glass light above her was actually a skylight, allowing the city's lights to filter in. She washed her hands, then gently touched a couple of polished stones on a narrow shelf below the mirror. A black opal that reminded her of a mood ring, ready to shine with streaks of different colors. A plain gray pebble shaped similar to a lopsided heart. And her favorite, which held a fossilized leaf imprint.

Did Chad collect cool-looking rocks in his pockets when he went out on a walk, taking them home?

She exited the bathroom after drying her hands on possibly the plushest towel she'd ever laid fingers upon. Following a clattering sound, she passed a spacious living room with cozy-looking couches piled with worn, sun-faded cushions.

To her right she found Chad, standing with his back to her in a dazzling kitchen of her dreams. A white quartz gigantic island sat in the middle, and a half a dozen stools lined up on the sitting room side. There were no walls between the two areas and she could only imagine how amazing the natural light must be during the day.

The beautiful island top was bare, the usual assorted junk that tended to accumulate on kitchen counters strangely absent. However, built into the island's side were three shelves, where a dark brown basket spilled over with miscellanea. Everything from phone charger cords, papers and other common necessities nobody knew how to organize.

Below that was a haphazard stack of cookbooks. The top one looked well-thumbed, the edges stained, the book puffed up because of wrinkled pages. The cookbook was hers, and it was not, by the looks of things, being used as a doorstop as she'd erroneously assumed.

She gently pulled it from the pile, keeping her eyes on Chad, who still had his back to her as he filled a glass at the sink. To his left and right was a who's-who lineup of kitchen gadgets and electronics. An air fryer, mixer, blender, slow cooker, bread machine… Everything you could buy and plug in seemed to be there. And they were no longer perfectly pristine, either.

Athena flipped open her cookbook and skimmed the margin's handwritten notes. It was clear why Chad asked such intelligent questions during their video filming.

Chad Mullens cooked. And he used her recipes.

She didn't know this man at all.

And for some reason, she really liked that idea.

* * *

Mullens said nothing as Athena gently closed her cookbook and set it back on the shelf.

"Thought you might be thirsty," he said, sliding a fresh glass of water toward her.

"Thanks." She perched on a stool, taking in his kitchen. "Nice and big."

"Are you talking about my kitchen or something else?"

She choked on a sip of water, then sent him an exasperated look. He could have sworn that beneath it a smile was fighting to break through.

"The only way to get the best kitchen is to buy the penthouse," he joked.

"You know, that's exactly what I told my real estate agent," she said over the rim of her glass.

"Did not." He shook his head at her, and her playful smirk grew. He tapped the countertop. "Want the tour?"

Athena shrugged, feigning indifference, but he detected a hint of eagerness to do a bit of snooping.

"Follow me."

Normally, he didn't invite people back to his house, and if he did, they certainly didn't get a grand tour. But even though it was risky, he wanted her to see his home, and possibly break some of her assumptions about him.

She set down her glass and dutifully followed as he gestured to his slightly dumpy wraparound couch and the navy shag area rug that had been a dumb idea. His current vacuum cleaner could never quite get all the popcorn bits out of it. "Living room."

They crossed the space and entered the other half of the penthouse where there were four bedrooms, two more bathrooms, his workout area plus access to his private rooftop patio.

Mullens gestured to the left. "Bathroom." She peeked her head inside. Then he opened the first door on the right and allowed it to swing open. "Guest room. If you're too tired to go home tonight—or any night—you're always welcome to stay."

"Won't cramp your style?"

"Me and my date don't have to come back here."

Athena snorted in amusement and stared into the guest room, her eyes narrowing, hands moving to rest on her curvy hips. "Is that a floral bedspread?"

He laughed, having forgotten how incongruent it was with his public image. His first roommate after moving out of his dad's house had definitely ridden him hard about that flowery bedcover. "Grandma made it."

He went to close the door again, but Athena stepped inside, smoothing a hand over the soft, worn fabric. The quilt was colorful, an abundance of small squares stitched together by hand. When he'd been born, his grandmother had collected bits of cloth from relatives, making something that wove him into the fabric of a family that no longer gathered, was no longer held together by the threads of their mutual bloodline.

"It's beautiful." Athena turned, her expression changing from delight to that curious one she got when she was about to probe him. "Is she gone? Your grandma?"

He nodded, the lump in his throat restricting him from saying anything. He moved to the next door, expecting she'd follow, and swung it open when she caught up. "Office."

The pale green room with the maple flooring was simply furnished with a desk and a chair. Shades were drawn across the large, south-facing window and they waved slightly as the air-conditioner regulated the temperature.

The next room hadn't exactly been described as one in the real estate listing, as it had no actual doors. The corner of the building, where two outer walls met, each lined with a bank of floor-to-ceiling windows, created a den area. Mullens had fitted the space with rubber workout flooring. His treadmill and bike were set in front of the windows, and a TV and sound system were at the ready to keep his mind occupied while his body worked. On a sunny day, biking in front of all that glass, it felt like he was in the sky, defeating the laws of gravity, like a bicycling Superman.

Along the inner wall his weight rack and some of his other favorite torture devices sat waiting. This was one of the few places in his home that showed evidence of his career choice, thanks to the framed posters of himself in hockey gear hanging above the racks and beside the large mirrors. They served as motivation on days when his mind and body begged him to skip a workout.

Mullens hustled Athena along before she could spy the posters and crack a joke about his ego. "We're going in a bit of a circle here," he said, heading toward the end of the room and the west bank of windows. The night stretched out at his feet as he ducked through the next doorway to his left.

Athena stopped before the doorway. She stood close to the windows, her feet away from the edge of the room, the earth many stories below as she leaned her face toward the glass to peer downward. "Do you ever get scared you're going to walk through a window and fall to your death?"

"You afraid of heights?"

She straightened. "No! It's just..." She gazed at the tall windows, tentatively reaching out and pressing on the glass.

Mullens made a fist, leaned back through the doorway. He hammered on the thick pane in front of her. "See? No wobble. No cracks."

"Oh my gosh! Stop!" She jumped at him, grabbing his fist and pulling it down.

He drew his arm back to his side, bringing her with it. She went to release him and he lifted his arm again as though ready to knock.

"Chad!" she squealed, the danger and fear mixed with a thrill, leaving her dancing eyes a deep hazel.

"Do you sleepwalk?" he asked.

"What? No."

"Good. Because there are windows in my bedroom, too."

"You are so overly confident!" Athena complained. There was no way she'd acknowledge the little thrill that had zipped through her body like a bullet after hearing his implied offer that she could sleep in his room—with him.

"What do you mean?" Chad asked, a picture of innocence.

"You *know* what I mean."

"Tina!" He stepped back with fake surprise. "I am more than just a sex symbol."

She rolled her eyes, her unease at walking through the playboy's bedroom replaced by exasperation. Although "exasperation" wasn't quite right. Amusement, maybe? A feeling of unexpected adventure? Or satisfaction that even though she was a book nerd with lots of food rules, Chad still found her woman enough to flirt with?

He flirts with everyone, she reminded herself. She shook her head slightly, realizing that what she felt most right now was comfort and trust. Maybe even some weird, possibly misplaced sense of belonging.

Chad waved toward his en suite as he crossed his bedroom toward the door on the far side. To their right the windows had changed, no longer starting at the floor but just above knee height, and power shades had been drawn from the top downward so a gap of glass was exposed near the ceiling.

"You're not an exhibitionist?" She gestured to the covered panes. "Somehow that's surprising, but also reassuring."

"Who says I'm not?" He grinned from the doorway, clearly eager to have her continue on. It made her want to stop and absorb even more, feeling intensely curious about what she might find in the most private room of his home. She might not ever have another excuse to nose around in here, plus there was the fact that he wanted to keep moving, which increased her desire to study everything in sight.

He'd been touchy about the homemade blanket in the guest suite, and it appeared anything to do with family closed him up like a vault.

His bed had a massive headboard, a nondescript comforter and one pillow on the left side. One. He had a bedside table, but again, just one.

"Are those walk-in closets?" She itched to open the doors flanking the king-size bed. The man had style, and she bet each space was chock-full of goodies. NHL players tended to dress in designer suits on their way to and from games, but Chad took it to another level with his one-of-a-kind flair.

"Do monkeys eat bananas?" Chad stepped from the doorway to open the closet nearest him. She peeked inside, then entered. It was bigger than most children's bedrooms and the track lighting illuminated rows of suits, racks of perfectly lined up shoes, several tie racks, and hats resting on shelves above.

The colors. The fabrics. She longed to sit on the small bolster by the shiny shoes and beg him to put on a fashion show.

At the far end of the room was a staging area with several open garment bags hanging on hooks, and designer suitcases on a low table waiting to be filled. It was clear the man had a system. With so many away games each season, it was smart to leave things laid out in a way that didn't mean tripping over a suitcase all the time.

She looked around for the jeans, jerseys, workout gear and sweaters she often saw him in. There were a few drawers, but they were smaller, suitable for items such as socks and trays of cufflinks. His casual wear wasn't kept in here.

"All you wear are suits?" she asked.

"The other closet has my day-to-day items." He pointed to an adjoining door in the corner that linked the two closets. It was closed, like most doors in his house, and she wondered why he didn't leave them open.

"What will you do if you get married?"

"She can put her stuff in the guest room."

Athena laughed, and he rewarded her with a small smile.

She paused on her way out of the closet, recognizing a few items on the rack labeled Cleaners. She fingered the baby blue ruffled tuxedo shirt he'd worn to the gala, surprised he hadn't had it laundered immediately after the whiskey incident.

"You wore this well," she said. "Not even an ironic whiff of pimp daddy."

His eyes met hers, amusement crinkling the flesh bracketing his mouth. She felt a tremor start at her feet and work its way through her nervous system. The room was suddenly too small, too closed in, too private.

"Even though it should have been burned in the seventies," she added in an offhand tone.

"Hey! That was custom-made." He tapped the sleeve she was holding, breaking her grip on the fabric.

Giggling, she took another look at the shirt and its neighboring tuxedo jacket and pants. "You paid to have that made?"

Chad lowered his eyebrows and heaved a sigh, opened his mouth and then closed it again. He turned to leave, then turned back.

"Sorry?" she asked innocently. "Did you want to say something?"

"What are the odds of me finding a tux from that era that fits all of this?" He gestured to his thick quads and the way his jeans stretched tight over them. Mouthwatering.

She shrugged, making her eyes big and doubtful.

"And anyway," he grumbled, "didn't you have *your* dress made?"

She laughed. "You must think they pay me a lot more than they do." She shook her head. "Consignment shop that specializes in designer items."

"Huh. Good find."

"Thanks." She'd had to let out the gown in several areas, but thankfully there'd been enough material that she'd been able to do so.

"Very jazz lounge," he said, scanning her curves as though imagining her in the dress again.

"I was thinking blues."

"Yeah, I could see that."

Their fingers touched while reaching for the light switch, and Chad let his hand linger over hers, the light from the bedroom casting his face in a soft warm glow.

She wanted to step closer, lean into him and press her lips to his.

* * *

Mullens thought Athena was going to kiss him. But then she shot past him, ducking under his arm and exiting the bedroom like her underwear was on fire.

"It's getting late," she said. "I should go."

He caught her hand, slowing her. "We're not done the tour."

"Chad…"

"One more thing. And I think you'll get a kick out of it."

She dropped her shoulders and sagged.

"Come on, trust me, Tina."

He opened yet another door, near the entry where they'd come in only twenty minutes ago.

Athena's jaw slackened and he let go of her hand as she moved into the room as though pulled by a magnet. His home library. Bookcases took up the two side walls and two perfectly broken-in, cozy armchairs faced a fireplace. Coffee table. A few plants and a forgotten bottle of water.

"You read?" She turned to him, eyes wide.

"Most people do, Tina."

She shook her head. "No, they don't. And they sure don't have an entire room dedicated to it."

"Well, I don't have kids. Had to fill the room somehow."

He watched as she ran her fingers reverently along a row of book spines, pausing to tap a few, take a couple out to check the covers. Her sudden need to leave had evaporated like dew on a Texas summer morning. She headed to a stack on the table beside an armchair and picked up the hardcover on top, a biography. "This what you're reading right now?"

"One of several." Obviously, she hadn't noticed the books on his bedside table. Or on the coffee table in the living room. It was one of the dangers of living alone. You had to fill the space and time somehow.

She flipped it open to where his bookmark rested, and skimmed a few paragraphs. "Hmm. You're at the best part."

"Don't spoil it for me."

"Never." She set the book down again.

After several minutes she left the room with what sounded like a whispered promise to return.

"One more thing," he said. He doubled back the way they'd come, skipping over a door they'd passed when she'd wanted to flee, minutes ago.

"What's in here?" She paused in front of it.

"Storage mostly." The space had basically become a dumping ground, and was extra awful at the moment thanks to boxes of Christmas decorations he'd pulled out, then hadn't had the heart to put up last month.

"Dead bodies?" she asked, keeping one eye on him as she opened the door. She glanced away, taking in the room. "Oh." Disappointment filled her voice, and she closed the door again.

"But check this out." He moved to the far end of the

hallway near his bedroom to what appeared to be a segment of opaque windows and pressed one of the glass panels.

She gasped when it slid open. "A secret door?" Athena was at his side in a flash, delicately dancing her fingertips down the glass pieces before stepping into the humid room.

When he'd moved in, he'd had the area closed in to trap the humidity and heat from the greenhouse he'd had built at the top of the staircase that led to his private rooftop patio.

Athena climbed onto the first step, gaping at the water feature that stretched upward to the floor above.

She turned to him, her eyes wild, like a child who'd had too much sugar. "Do you have another secret door in your library? Maybe behind a shelf?" She stepped off the staircase as though ready to go back and look for one.

He smiled at her enthusiasm and shook his head, happy for the first time that he'd been traded to the Dragons.

"Have you checked? Because maybe a secret bookshelf doorway pops out into your suit closet!" She frowned, chewing on her bottom lip. "No, wait. That's not a shared wall, is it?"

"It would be pretty cool to have a bookshelf door, but alas, no secret passageways that I'm aware of."

"You're one colossal disappointment, Chadwick." She turned and headed up the staircase. "Where are we going?"

"The roof." The stairs led them past the trickling curtain of water to their right, ivy growing up alongside. A tall, narrow window stretched from floor to ceiling and beyond, merging into the glass-domed greenhouse on the rooftop.

Because it was dark out, he flicked on the lights, ensuring he also turned on the colored ones that lit up the water feature.

"I want to live here," Athena declared as she climbed.

"That could be arranged," he said, experiencing a strange, stabbing yearning in his chest. He rubbed the spot as though he could push out the loneliness that came with the feeling.

The top of the stairs deposited them onto a landing and the greenhouse where he was growing herbs and vegetables. He winced, doubting the wisdom of bringing her up here.

The gig was up with his eating and cooking habits, but when she saw his garden he figured things could go one of two ways. She could either rage at him for his duplicity and mockery, or else see the real him, a man she could reject for simply not having enough substance to care about.

He wasn't sure which was scarier.

"Pardon the mess," he said, moving past her to open the greenhouse door, turning on more lights as he went. The grow lights behind him were illuminating what a slovenly gardener he was. Spilled dirt, dead leaves, containers of rotting compost, and discarded buckets littered the glassed-in room.

Silently Athena followed him out onto the rooftop patio, where the air was welcoming and cool. Above, strings of lights lit up the outdoor living space shaded by wide umbrellas. Potted palms, wicker couches and outdoor rugs made the area look less rooftop and more cozy. The small fountains, fans and misters were off, but in the heat of the day they worked to keep the area a reasonable temperature so he could sit up here without frying.

"That's the tour."

Athena was silent for a long moment, then turned to him, her face awash with delight in the magical light of the patio.

And this time he was dead certain she was going to kiss him.

* * *

"Will you cook for me?"

"What?" Chad looked adorably thrown off as their bodies drifted closer together.

"Cook me your favorite recipe in that amazing kitchen of yours."

"How about I kiss you instead?" He lowered his lips, grazing hers in a way that knocked her off-kilter, awakening her body with an electric buzz.

She rested her palms against his firm chest, pressing her mouth harder to his. Their tongues touched, and his hands slid down her back to her butt in what felt like ownership. She gasped against his lips and the kiss turned hotter.

Athena jerked and pushed away, realizing this was all a tactic. A ploy to draw her further from him, the real him. Re-centering herself, her eyes caught on his tattoo. "What does this mean?" she asked, reaching for the inked skin.

He turned his head, chin down, as though wanting to hide the few leaves that showed above the neck of the black sweater that hugged his muscles, putting them on display even while covering them with fine wool. "Nothing much."

"*Chad...*"

"I just like the way it looks."

His lips were on hers again and her mind blanked, her body taking over the conversation. His arms felt so right wrapped around her, his strong hands gliding over her rib cage. She sighed against his mouth.

When they came up for air she realized she'd been sucked into another wonderful kiss.

"Tell me something about you," she whispered, stroking a

finger down his cheekbone and through the hollow above his wonderful jaw. "Something personal."

"Tina…" His lips were lowering to hers again.

"No." She wasn't falling for a distracting kiss a second time. She turned her head away, one hand on his chest. "Why, Chad?"

He licked his lips, appearing wary when she dared peek up at him. "Why what?"

"Why won't you let me in?"

His body loosened and his limbs relaxed as he released her. Then he stepped back into her space, angling for another kiss. "I think I just did."

"No." Her breath hitched in her throat, torn between want and need. "You have this wall." She slapped a hand flat against his pecs, just above his heart. "You kiss me instead of showing me you can cook. You deny that you follow the rules and eat based on the plan, and you deny *me* to the point of mockery. And to make it even worse, you think you can blind me from all that by giving me a kiss."

"I—"

"You won't talk about your family. You hustled me through your house like I'm too dumb to notice whenever I got close to discovering something that might actually tell me who you are." She pushed on his chest again, trying to shake him into reacting. Something. Anything.

"I'm sorry." He remained unyielding, unapologetic despite his words.

"What are you afraid of?"

He blinked, his mouth opening, his gaze falling away. "Me?"

She waited for the words that might explain.

"No, Tina… I…"

"And why can't you call me by my actual name? Is that too scary for you? Too intimate or personal?"

He didn't have an answer, simply stood with his hands at his sides, looking lost.

She shook her head. "I'm sorry. I can't do this. Not with you."

He caught her hand as she turned to leave. "Don't go."

"We were both playing tonight, and it was fun, but we've been ignoring the truth. *I've* been ignoring it."

"My image is just that, Tina. It's not real. That's not who I am. That's the guy who sells stuff. Cars, aftershave. Not me."

"I know that. That's not what I'm talking about." She was in the space between. Between the image and reality. And he had the real man locked up so tight she couldn't even find the bread crumbs that might lead her to him.

She really thought she might like that man. Love him, even.

"You're not ready." She gently pressed a hand against his chest, a wave of sorrow washing over her at the thought that she'd have no excuse after tonight to feel the strong ripple of muscles under his fabulous sweaters. "I'll never know you. You'll never let me close enough for something real. The kind of real I need."

CHAPTER 9

Mullens walked down the long cinderblock hallway, joking with Leo Pattra as they made their way to the locker room to gear up for practice.

"You should move to Sweetheart Creek," his teammate said, immediately sending Mullens' cheery mood plummeting.

"Why?"

"You spend enough time there."

Not any longer. Athena had made it clear after that kiss where she'd branded his soul that she was not interested in damaged, baggage-ladened men. The club in which he was the original card-carrying member.

"Says who?" he asked.

"I've seen you there."

"Yeah? Well, why don't *you* move there?"

"I will if you will?" Leo said with a grin.

"I have a feeling you're going to be getting married and settling down there," Mullens stated meaningfully. "Long before I could even convince any of the town's residents to give me a shot."

"Yeah, Violet and I had some bumps. Now it's just the good kind." He gave another goofy grin and Mullens playfully shoved him into the wall.

Leo laughed. "We need to find you someone. Maybe there's a geriatric dating service. Tinder for the infirm."

"Save the old-people jokes for Maverick and Dylan."

"Did I hear my name?" Dylan O'Neill asked, jogging up behind them.

"I'm setting you two up on Elderly Tinder."

Dylan snorted. "I have a girlfriend."

"Who? Jenny?" Leo nearly doubled over with laughter. "Keep dreaming, pal."

"From Sweetheart Creek? That Jenny?" Mullens asked. It felt as if his teammates were easily sliding into a domestic life, falling in love and making Sweetheart Creek their home without effort. Some people were like that—at home no matter where they went. Seeing it happen to his teammates left Mullens feeling hollow and lacking.

"Yeah. Owns Blue Tumbleweed. Friends with your arch enemy Gavras," Leo said, stopping outside the locker room door.

Athena. How did it all go so badly again?

"But Jenny *hates* Dylan," Leo continued. "They fight like cats and dogs."

Dylan was shaking his head, looking skyward. "We're not enemies. She thinks I'm great."

"She thinks you're great as roadkill, you mean?" Leo snickered, and Dylan shoved the door open, almost hitting Louis Bellmore, who was coming out.

The coach stepped back, out of the way, then lifted his chin as Mullens passed. "Meet me in my office?"

"Now?"

Coach nodded. He recrossed the locker room to his adjoining office, meaning he'd been looking for him. Not good.

Mullens followed, stopping by his locker to drop his bag. Leo and Dylan bickered all the way to their own lockers, making him chuckle. But as he passed Landon's locker on his way to the office, where the coach was waiting in the doorway, the goalie lifted his eyebrows and smirked. "You slept with the wrong woman this time, Mullens!"

Once the others realized Mullens had been summoned, hoots and laughter filled the room.

"Better eat some vegetables, Mullens, 'cause you're about to get canned like peas!"

"Your jokes suck, Dylan!" Mullens retorted, turning to point at him before Louis closed his office door behind them, dulling the din.

"Have a seat." He gestured to the chair across from his desk.

"What's up?" Mullens asked, folding himself into the crappy chair. Maybe if they won some cups Louis could get chairs with better padding.

"I chose you as my number-one pick."

Mullens head snapped up. "Say that again?"

"I chose you."

He'd been chosen? He hadn't been force-traded, unloaded or rejected?

"You were my long shot. My Moby Dick. I figured if I had you, I had a chance at the playoffs." Louis sat on the edge of his desk, his hands clasped in his lap.

"Moby Dick?" he asked, forcing down the feeling of failure. It had been up to him to lead, and he hadn't.

"The big catch. The unattainable what-if. The one that keeps you up at night and haunts your dreams."

"I don't think that's the theme of *Moby Dick*."

Louis leaned forward. "Except now you're going to kill me, my career, my team. Very *Moby Dick*."

Mullens shifted uncomfortably, not appreciating the heavy stack of guilt Coach had just dropped on him. If he'd known he'd been specially selected, would he have acted any differently? No. He was doing his best. It's just that his best, all the way from his personal life to his career, wasn't enough.

"What I didn't expect was this huge chip on your shoulder." Louis sat back, arms crossed. "Your previous coaches all said great things about your discipline, but where diet comes into play, I haven't seen that."

"I'm sorry I failed you, Coach."

Louis was silent for a long moment. "Do I need to let her go?"

Mullens' heart beat faster. "Who?"

"Don't be coy. Athena Gavras."

He shook his head. "She's great."

"Yeah? That's strange, seeing as you sure as heck aren't listening to her—despite her credentials and expertise."

Mullens kept his head lowered, unsure what to say. To Athena. To Coach Bellmore.

"Do yourself a favor. Go to the bookstore down the street, grab all of her cookbooks and learn from them."

"She only has one."

"What?"

"Her second cookbook comes out in March. I'm on the cover."

Louis blinked. "You?"

"And I am following the diet plan, sir."

He scoffed. "She struck you from her roster last month for being uncooperative. And don't think I didn't hear about you crumpling up her pancake recipe on day one, and her throwing a drink on you at the gala."

"What?" There had been no throwing of drinks. The most that had happened was that he'd spilled his watered-down apple juice on her when he'd gone to catch her.

This was a bigger mess to unravel than he'd realized. He stretched back in his chair, wishing he could get himself traded and start fresh somewhere else. It sure would be easier right about now.

"Do you wanna see my binder of recipes with the stains on them?" he offered. "I follow her diet."

"So it's a personality conflict?"

Mullens shook his head.

"You slept with her?"

He frowned, showing his disapproval at the question.

"What?" Louis shrugged. "She's cute."

Mullens growled at the thought of the other man checking her out. Athena wasn't just cute. She was gorgeous, smart and strong-minded. She was exactly the kind of woman he'd be proud to take home to meet his family, if there was anything left of it.

"So it's pride then? You can't take instructions from a woman?"

"I take instructions from Karlene," he pointed out, referring to the team's physical therapist.

"So it's Athena?" Louis seemed conflicted.

"No, sir. She's great."

"You're not happy here?"

"No, I am," he said, realizing with surprise that it was true.

"So, what do you need from me?"

"Nothing. I'm good." He jiggled his legs, ready to suit up and get on the ice for practice.

"Then do me a favor and show up at your meetings with her, be respectful, follow the diet plan and call her by her real name."

"I am. I will."

He'd obviously let his own problems dominate his life for much too long. He should have manned up, apologized to Athena immediately after their first meeting and set things right. He hadn't done that.

Even worse was that he wanted her to date him. After all that? What was wrong with him?

"I don't call her Tina to be mean," he explained. He needed that distance, because calling her by her real name felt too intimate. It felt like stepping off a cliff and realizing there was nothing below to catch him. Just free-falling.

"Fine. But it obviously annoys her. So stop. And get the other guys on board. Clean up their diet, clean up their attitudes and be the role model I hired you to be. Lead this team into some wins." Louis stood up, indicating the meeting was over.

Mullens sighed, resting his elbows on his knees. Louis made it all sound so simple.

"Come on, man," Coach said, stepping toward the door. "It's either figure it out or I have to start shuffling people."

Mullens couldn't move, his thoughts stuck in neutral.

"I don't know what to do to help," Louis said, "and I don't want to lose either of you. But the dynamic is clearly not working. I'm going to need to provide feedback in her exit interview."

"No. Don't fire her." He shook his head. "It's me. When I'm around her, I..." His throat closed up.

"What? Feel anger? Resentment? Oppositionally defiant?" Louis seemed amused.

Mullens looked up, meeting his coach's gaze, hoping the man could read him, fix him, make it all better—without him having to say a word.

"Well?" Coach prompted, suddenly somber.

"I feel like she might have the power to break me."

* * *

"The channel went live!" Athena couldn't look away from her online cooking show.

She already had three subscribers, herself, Meddy and their mom. Their dad was afraid of the internet or she'd have four.

She needed to post a sign in the Huckleberry Bookshop once it opened to ask people to subscribe—and maybe spam all the guys on the team and tell them to as well.

"Chad! It's live!" she called through her open office doorway, causing the man to stop.

He peeked around the corner. "Say what?"

"We're famous!" She swiveled her computer monitor to face him. He came in, hunching slightly to get a better angle on the screen.

"Look at that," he said. "Let me subscribe."

She waited while he played with his phone, then hit Refresh on her browser. She squealed. "Four!"

"You playing golf, cutie?" He perched on the edge of her desk, his mind clearly elsewhere. Or maybe this was small beans and boring to someone with his level of fame.

"Sorry. Just a little excited." She put her computer to sleep and turned to face him more fully, but he was back on his phone.

With a jolt Athena came crashing down to earth, realizing that the last time they'd spoken she'd shut him down. She'd called him out on the walls he erected to keep her out, and told him he wasn't real enough to be her boyfriend. And now she was acting like they were buddies.

And maybe they sort of were, even though they didn't have what it took to start a solid relationship.

Chad pocketed his phone and looked at her as if he couldn't quite figure her out.

"Still friends?" she asked quietly, her heart racing in her chest.

He stood. "No."

"Oh."

At the door, he turned. "I'll never settle for that. You know I want more."

She shivered, knowing he was a man who was used to getting what he wanted.

"Chad, I told you I need—"

"Something real. That you need to *know* me."

"Yes!"

"Maybe some guys don't talk with words, Tina."

"Seriously! My name is Athena!"

"Maybe you already know me. Ever consider that?" He vanished out the door, and she sighed, his words running circles in her tired mind.

She went back to work, her thoughts everywhere but on her dietary plans and tracking sugar levels for her diabetic player. Unable to focus, she finally closed the document and checked her watch. Time to go home to the store.

Athena gently rubbed her eyes, unable to wait to take out her contact lenses and give her eyes a break. She was crazy. She was working too hard and was going to wake up in her fifties and realize it was too late to have the dreams she'd assumed were hers. Dreams like finding love and having a family.

She hit the lights and locked her office, bumping into Chad at a hallway junction. He waved his phone. "Two hundred and thirty-five."

"What?"

"Subscribers."

"What? No! Already?" She grabbed her own phone, checking for herself. There'd only been the four of them when they'd been chatting twenty minutes ago. She looked at the screen, blinked, read it again. "Two hundred and forty-four!"

That was a dizzying number of subscribers in such a short period of time. Far too many to all be family and friends.

"I posted about it on social." Chad winked and turned, leaving her there to obsess over how fast the numbers were crawling upward—and all thanks to him.

CHAPTER 10

What on earth was Armadillo Day? Mullens wandered among the revelers on Main Street, Sweetheart Creek. The evening parade had ended, and he'd lost sight of Athena and Meddy. They'd been handing out mini tarts and grinning like their dreams were coming true. They'd been working the crowds without having to check in with each other, always knowing where the other sister was and what they needed. More huckleberry tarts? The other sister was already approaching the car driven by what Mullens guessed was their dad, and grabbing another tray from their mother, who was in the backseat.

It made Mullens homesick for a life that no longer existed for him. After Evonne had passed away, his parents had split, and he'd shuttled between the two homes, often forgotten about. There were no family meals or trips, just notes on containers of food in the fridge, or pinned to cash and left on the counter along with a takeout menu. And so he'd learned to cook as well as how to count on himself.

Eventually his dad had bought him a car so he could drive himself to hockey practices or take himself to games and tournaments. Next had come a credit card, and lies about his age when hotel clerks asked for an accompanying adult, or ID proving that he was one, in order to check in during out-of-town tournaments.

Somehow, despite a lack of parental guidance, Mullens had achieved his dreams.

But he'd never really gotten past his grief, had he? Never really figured out the pain.

He stood on the corner, blindly watching the small town go by, people nodding to him, offering hellos. Just a stranger, and yet he felt like he was at home.

Before he could change his mind he pulled his phone from his back pocket and dialed the team's psychologist.

"Hey, it's Mullens."

"What's up?" The man on the other end of the line was kind, but also had a firm edge that said don't-mess-with-me. He'd tried to crack Mullens a time or two; he'd been making the rounds through the Dragons since September.

Miranda, the team's owner, had a plan to whip her players into shape, everything from being more financially aware to dealing with their own emotional baggage, as well as taking care of their nutrition and physical fitness. He'd never been on a team quite like the Dragons, and he found it was growing on him. It wasn't just a job; it was a family and everything that went along with it.

Doubting himself, he remained silent.

"Mullens?"

He caught sight of Athena hustling across the street, beelining it to the bookstore. Tonight was the grand opening and he'd caught only glimpses of her all week as she prepared for it.

"I was thinking…" he began.

Athena looked tired. Had she stopped to eat today? He'd tried pressing a cup of apple cider into her hands earlier—after sidestepping an armadillo that seemed intent on keeping a cluster of people away from the food trucks. Apparently, the beast didn't understand that the day was in its honor—or maybe it did and was lording it over the humans. But getting Athena to accept the drink had been like forcing a cat into a travel carrier.

"Mullens?"

"Sorry." He closed his eyes, pinched the bridge of his nose and turned away from the street. "I was thinking I have some stuff I haven't let go of. Can you help me with that?"

"Yes." There was a pause. "When are you free?"

Mullens faltered. "Now?"

The man laughed. "I'm eating supper with my family. The only reason I didn't let your call go to voice mail is because I imagined you might be desperate."

"I am."

His tone turned to wary concern. "Is it urgent?"

Mullens watched Athena vanish into her shop, her words from the other week rattling in his head about how he didn't let her in—and he knew that was because he was avoiding feeling the pain of his past.

"Not life or death, but I'm ready to make a change."

* * *

Athena had been operating on adrenaline and excitement, but she could feel her energy starting to wane. It had been a long week. The shop was now open and people were streaming in for tonight's grand opening, keeping her and Meddy hopping.

And Chad was everywhere.

He had been since the kiss. Like a stray, it felt as though he was always lurking in the shadows, one eye on her in case she set out another food dish. Or in their situation, let down her guard and opened herself to another kiss.

She'd thought about that kiss a lot. Too much.

She wanted more. She also wanted to spend time with Chad in his fabulous home, curled up for days, poking about, getting to know him. Seeing exactly what was growing in that garden of his, and having fun cooking together.

But he was still closed up, hiding whatever it was he had in his heart. And, sadly, it wasn't going to open up just because she wanted it to.

Speak of the devil. When she turned from delivering a cappuccino to a customer, Chad was standing in the bookshop's doorway.

He looked different than he had earlier. Resolved, somehow, in a way that sent a shiver of anticipation zigzagging through her spine.

And yet that alpha energy he carried was more peaceful than usual, as though he'd made a decision about something that had been weighing on him.

Holding his gaze, she moved back behind the counter to make a decaf tea latte for her cousin Hannah, who was browsing through the children's books with her two boys.

"Tina," Chad said, giving her a nod.

She rolled her eyes in exasperation.

The day he called her by her real name was the day she'd forgive him and let it all go. The day she'd kiss him like she meant it.

Good thing that would never happen.

He tipped his chin in her direction. "Two thousand and eighty-nine."

She sprinkled cinnamon sugar on top of the finished latte's foamed milk, waving Hannah over. She took a sip of her own coffee while considering the new subscriber number. It had gone way up, with the views and comments on their first cooking video numbering the thousands. It was a smash hit. At least by her standards.

Chad wandered through the shop, and she watched him while she helped customers, curious where he'd pause. Philosophy? Sports? Crime fiction? Would he sit in one of the chairs in the back section with a couple of hockey books to see if he was mentioned in any of them? If so, he should choose the big blue hardcover first.

"Hey, hot stuff!" Meddy called out to him. "Everything is 15 percent off tonight."

"Thanks, Meddy."

Her sister beamed, no doubt feeling the power of his unwavering gaze—the one where it felt like there was nobody else he'd rather be talking to. Nobody else that mattered in that moment.

"Love the shirt, by the way."

"Couldn't resist." Chad glanced down at his navy blue Armadillo Day sweatshirt, one Athena knew was part of the fundraising efforts Brant and April Wylder had undertaken in order to build the town its first official animal shelter.

His eyes shifted, locking on Athena's as he blasted her with a full-beam smile that rocked her. "You like it?"

It was tucked into his belted jeans and the fabric bulged out in the front as though he'd stuffed something down inside —a major style faux pas and very anti-Chad. His midriff wiggled and the ugliest little head popped out of the neck hole, licking Chad's chin.

"Is that a puppy?"

"That Brant guy asked me to hold him while he managed a Great Dane. I think he's trying to get Landon to—"

"No pets in the store."

"What about Clem?" He pointed to the cat's basket, now moved to a short shelf of travel books. The poor feline wasn't so sure about the invasion of people tonight, and had slipped out, hopefully to return later.

"He's the landlord," Athena replied. "Doesn't count."

Chad chuckled.

"Aw, this cute little sad puppy has to stay," Meddy said, going over to pet the dog's shaved head. It shivered in anticipation of meeting someone new, then ducked back into Chad's sweatshirt before she could make contact. Hannah's boys, Thomas and Wade, swarmed the hockey player, eager to see the puppy, but it remained hidden.

"He seems pretty shy," Chad explained to them. "Had a rough life. Brant said he was so matted he had to fully shave him, and had to stitch him up along his hip, too."

"We have customers, Meddy," Athena muttered, walking past with a huckleberry tart and latte for a customer sitting at the window overlooking Main Street. "And Travis would like another beer and Donna needs another glass of white." She gestured to the table where the town's former mayor and his wife were sitting, chatting with friends and enjoying the liquor license acquired for the store's grand opening.

"See you at next weekend's game," Meddy said, waving to Chad as she skipped behind the counter.

Athena's gut tightened with dread as she thought about next

Saturday. Not only had her ex, Lonnie, reached out via text to meet up for a quick chat before his New Jersey team took on the Dragons, but she'd forgotten her promise to Meddy. Her sister had caught her in a weak moment, making her commit to finally taking advantage of her free Dragons passes. So a week from today the two of them would close up the store a touch early and head into the city with Jenny and Cassandra to watch a game.

Fun, right?

Sure. But right now all Athena wanted was to go home and sleep for a month.

Outside the shop's doors she caught a glimpse of Cassandra and Landon as their kids, Dusty and Rylnn, ripped in, full of energy. She smiled, delighted at how well five-year-old Dusty was doing. The kid had been through the medical wringer lately, and it was a relief to see it was turning out well for the young family.

"There are new Batman sticker books in the corner," she called to Dusty. "Princess ones, too," she added for Rylnn's benefit.

"Yes!" The girl skipped to the shelf in one of her ever-present, sparkling princess costumes.

Cass and Landon were talking out on the sidewalk and Athena went back to work, startled a few minutes later when the sound of applause filtered into her shop. What was happening out there? Were people crowding around Cass and Landon? She felt like she was missing out on everything lately. Always go, go, go. Once the cookbook was launched and the store established she needed to hire some help and spend more time with her friends again.

Rylnn and Dusty went scooting back outside, and that's when Athena noticed Chad in the kids' section by the door, sitting cross-legged on the floor. Not in the sports section, skimming hockey books as she'd expected.

She kept an eye on him as he flipped through books, laughing at some, discarding others as soon as he saw the cover. A stack was building beside him, and she was curious who the lucky recipient was going to be.

She thought about moseying by, but Hannah came to the counter with a book for each of her boys.

"How are your classes?" Athena asked as she rang her through. Her cousin had recently decided to go back to school, making her a very busy single mom.

Maybe keeping busy was a family trait and not an actual personality flaw, like some people believed.

"There's this one on child development and learning—Wade, quit poking Thomas—which is super interesting." She eyed the tub of dirty dishes behind Athena that was waiting to be taken into the kitchen. "Text me if you need help cleaning up tonight. I'm around."

"You've already done plenty." Hannah had spent hours making the back kitchen shine when she'd found out Athena would be shooting videos in the dusty space. Athena hadn't even had to bribe her with brownies.

"It's not every day you open a store!"

Hannah and the boys left and Athena's attention drifted back to Chad. He was watching a mother and child use sign language as the mom corraled two younger toddlers toward the bathroom at the rear of the store. Her signing child, who looked about four, settled in a beanbag chair with a giant sigh of resignation and began flipping through a picture book.

Chad leaned forward, catching the child's attention. He signed something and the child nodded, scooting closer. The child held the book while the hockey player told the story using his hands, pausing so the child could look at the illustrations before turning the next page.

Athena, absorbed in the sight, jerked when Henry Wylder asked her for a cup of decaf.

"You on drugs? You have a weird look on your face." Henry smoothed down his salt and peppery hair, then turned to look in the same direction she had been moments ago. "Well, hello!" he called to Chad, a smile cracking his leathery skin. "You been eating well again today? Mrs. Fisher's Saturday specials are a real treat over there at the diner, don'tcha think?"

Chad gave a sheepish half smile and said, "I missed it today."

"That's a real cryin' shame. I'm sure she has some pie left if you're fixin' for something sweet."

"Thanks."

Seriously? Chad Mullens had totally managed to charm the grumpy old curmudgeon? No wonder she was having issues holding her ground with the hunk. Apparently, she was the only one impervious to his charm.

Henry turned back to her with a harrumph, stating bluntly, "I never got one of those tarts you were handing out at the parade."

Technically, she'd served the last one a minute ago, but she reached under the counter and pulled a tart from the package reserved for her parents as thanks for their help and the loan of extra dishes for the grand opening. She set it on a clean plate and pushed it toward Henry. He was the kind of man who needed his wheels greased every so often so he didn't torture everyone. He'd fought the opening of her store in any way he could—just because he was Henry and she was creating change in the tiny town.

She poured a cup of decaffeinated coffee and handed it to him.

He had out his wallet, but he narrowed his eyes. "So I have to pay for a tart while everyone watching the parade got one for free? What kind of scam you got goin' on in here?"

"Those were parade treats!"

"She's not charging you, Henry!" Meddy laughed, leaning in front of Athena and pushing the plate closer to him. "Hon, this is on the house as our thanks for you running such a smooth parade earlier." She winked at him. "But don't you go expecting this special treatment every day, you ol' scallywag!"

Pink spots appeared on the man's cheeks and his jaw opened and closed a few times before he took his order and shuffled away.

"You need to teach me your dark magic tricks," Athena whispered in awe.

Her sister laughed. "It's called flirting. You should try it sometime." She elbowed Athena, then nodded meaningfully toward Chad.

He looked up and called, "How do you sign 'giraffe'? I can't remember."

Athena shrugged and the child's mom appeared around the corner of a bookcase with her twins, making a gesture.

"Thanks." Chad resumed reading.

Meddy said under her breath, "I like him."

"You don't know him."

"And you do, even with those blinders on?"

"What?" She turned in surprise.

"You assume he's another Lonnie, and he's totally not."

Athena considered that.

Truth? Yes.

Did she want to accept it? No, not really. Because if she did, then she might lose her heart.

She turned back to the espresso machine, shaking her head. Who was she kidding? Her heart had already packed its bags and was following Chad down the lane.

* * *

Mullens caught Athena yawning, her eyes tearing up as she did so. Outside, Armadillo Day had wound down, most of the booths on Main Street already dismantled and the food trucks either already gone or in the final stages of packing up.

He headed outside to collect several dishes that had been left on the two tables set on the sidewalk, keeping one hand cupped under the bundle of fur inside his sweatshirt. Next, he folded the sidewalk sign that announced the store's grand opening.

"Hey," Dylan O'Neill said, giving him a nod as he passed. His large black dog pulled on its leash hauling his teammate toward Mullens. "What are you doing in town? Didn't see you in the parade."

"I could ask the same of you."

Leo, the rookie, had walked in the parade alongside their team mascot, Dezzie. The big dragon costume was always worn by Leo's girlfriend, who lived in town. Mullens supposed it made sense that Violet should take part, but Leo? Why him?

Mullens leaned down to pet the dog, which squirmed and threw herself against his leg, knocking him back. A line of slobber pirouetted from the canine's mouth, streaking down his jeans.

"Fish, no!"

Mullens frowned. "Your dog's name is Fish?"

"I didn't name her. Brant Wylder did."

Brant. He'd failed to come back for his puppy. The one Fish had just discovered with her nose and was nudging insistently through the fabric of Mullens' sweatshirt. The small dog squirmed and Mullens turned away, trying to calm the pup. "You seen Brant?"

The puppy's head popped out the collar of Mullens' shirt, and Dylan laughed. "No, but if he gave you that dog, good luck in handing it back."

"What? No. I'm just holding him."

"You need to spend more time around here."

"I'm trying. But the rental listings Landon gave me were all out of date."

Dylan smirked and began tugging on his dog's leash. He lifted his chin. "Later."

"Yeah. Later." Mullens let his gaze track across the street and down to where Jenny Oliver's shop had closed up for the night, lights off. "Guess you're heading back to the city?"

"We'll see."

"A crusty bastard like you will never win over a sweetheart like Jenny." He grinned, waiting for Dylan to turn around and give him a one-finger salute. The man didn't disappoint.

Mullens let himself back into the store with the folded-up sign.

Earlier, Athena and Meddy's parents had been by the shop, their mother in a wheelchair. Now just their dad had returned, and was loading up boxes of what looked like dishes.

"I think they're closing up, son," Mr. Gavras said, his kind eyes the same deep hazel as Athena's.

"Thanks. Just seeing if Tina needs anything." His focus locked on the woman with the wavy brown hair.

"Athena," the older man corrected, darting a look at his daughter, who was hunched over some books and papers at the counter.

"Right. Sorry." Still cradling the puppy in his shirt, he leaned the sign against his leg and held out his free hand. "I'm Mullens."

Her dad gave him an apologetic look and shifted the box in his arms.

"Right! Sorry. Hands full." He inhaled, trying to calm himself and his sudden nerves. "Let me get the door." He ditched the sign and strode over, pushing open the door with one hand while supporting the puppy with the other.

"What have you got there?" Mr. Gavras asked, eyeing the squirming mass under the fabric while he passed.

"Apparently I got— Uh, it's a stray. Brant Wylder asked me to take care of it. But I haven't seen him around lately, so…I'm not sure what to do with it."

Mr. Gavras's smile widened knowingly.

"Did I inadvertently adopt a puppy?"

The man shrugged, giving him a look that was way too innocent.

If he had adopted the pup, could he even buy it food this late at night? A leash? A collar? Chew toys? What else did a puppy need? A bed? It could sleep on his—if it wasn't too high for the little guy to jump up onto.

Mullens followed Athena's dad to the car waiting on the street, then opened the hatch for him so he could set the boxes in the trunk. "Anything else to come out?"

"No, this is all." The man glanced back at the shop where

his daughters were still working. He stretched out his hand for Mullens to shake. "Thank you, Chad."

His first name hit him hard in the chest. Unable to speak, Mullens nodded, gave a firm shake, then returned to the bookstore on wooden legs.

Chad.

Why did Athena's dad know his first name? Did he follow hockey? Mullens somehow doubted that. But even if he did, the sports announcers always called him by his last name.

He paused inside the warm building filled with the scents of new books, coffee and pastries, wondering what had been said about him within the confines of the Gavras family. And if he was already in, or already out.

Athena looked up, large dark plastic circles framing her eyes at a haphazard angle.

She wore glasses. Gigantic frames that were way too big for her face.

They were perfect.

He longed to straighten them, and found himself moving closer, unable to look away as she blinked up at him from the pages of the book she was skimming, as if momentarily lost between two worlds. She was undeniably adorable.

As she pulled herself back to reality, closing the book and adding it to a stack beside her, Mullens could see into her like a window. Her hopes, her dreams. Her seriousness and pain were temporarily absent, and it was then that he knew Athena Gavras was the woman who finally had the power to break his heart.

* * *

Athena blinked and pushed away the books and paperwork stacked in front of her, watching as Chad grabbed a stool from behind her counter and set it across from her. The shop was closed, but he was still here. He'd hung around all evening, then helped with the cleanup without being asked. He wasn't going away despite the way she'd tried to shut things down between them at his apartment after their kiss. Kisses.

She wasn't sure if she loved his stubbornness or resented it.

It hadn't helped, seeing him use sign language to read stories to a child, while carrying that sad excuse for a puppy around in his sweatshirt. Her stupid ovaries were making their seahorse argument again.

Chad untucked his shirt, carefully transferring the small, sleeping puppy into the crook of his arm. He set Clem's basket on the floor, tucking the dog inside.

"This okay?" he asked.

Athena shrugged. The cat would probably hate having the smell of an unknown dog in his bed, but what was she going to do? Kick out the poor puppy or make Chad hold it even longer? Brant Wylder was up to something with this latest rescue. He didn't let just anyone babysit one of his animals. And where had the man vanished to?

Something was definitely up, and him leaving an animal with Chad was a bold statement. A statement of approval.

"So you know Brant?" she asked.

Chad shrugged. "Not especially." He'd returned to his stool, his elbows resting on the counter as he leaned forward.

"I'm heading out," Meddy called as she came through from the kitchen. "I have the dishwasher running, and I'll come in early to deal with the rest of the kitchen, as well as bake another few dozen muffins." She peered through the glass at the back of the treats case and frowned at the crumbs. Everything they'd made had been bought and eaten.

"We did good today." Athena stood, wrapping her sister in a hug.

"Just the beginning."

"Sure is."

Athena had believed that she'd eventually back away from the store and let Meddy buy her out. But the way they were tag-teaming problems, she kind of loved being so ensconced in her sister's life again—and in the community, too.

"See ya, cutie." Meddy winked at Chad.

He lifted a finger and angled his head downward as though tipping an invisible hat. "Later, Medusa."

She laughed at the nickname and headed for the back exit, and the outside stairs to her apartment above.

Chad slid off his stool again while Athena returned to hers, her feet throbbing after the number of steps she'd taken that day. She watched him cross the room, his strong body full of ease. He headed to the children's section, scooping up the stack of books he'd selected earlier. He set them in front of Athena, his credit card sitting on top.

"I donate money, my time, but also books." He reclaimed his spot on the stool across from her. His focus felt intense and, as a distraction from the heat pouring through her and the dwindling oxygen in her lungs, Athena started ringing up his purchases.

This irresistible hunk was one big mystery, wasn't he?

"The books go to an organization that helped my sister," he said, and Athena let that information settle inside her.

"That's why you know sign language?" She waited for the receipt to print, curious what more he'd reveal, if anything.

He nodded.

She thought for a moment, then decided to take a risk and walk through the conversational door he'd opened. "And she's why you know your way around a bobby pin and earrings? You helped out a lot?"

He nodded again.

"And why you carried that man in the wheelchair into the Dragons' headquarters when the ramp was out—you knew he was stuck?"

That one wasn't huge, though. Anyone half present would have put two and two together. It was more the way he'd taken charge, knowing he could carry the chair, man and all, up the stairs.

Chad nodded again, not looking up. She stilled, afraid to make a wrong move and have him close down or shut her out.

"She was a bit vain," he finally said in a low voice. "I used to tease her and call her Vainy. She loved it." His smile was wistful, etched with love but also pain.

"When did she pass away?"

His focus went to his thumbs, which did a little dance around each other as he hunched forward. "I was thirteen."

"That must've been hard."

He inhaled sharply, clearly uncomfortable, and Athena silently prayed that he'd trust her with his pain and stay with the thread of conversation. Open up to her.

"How did your family cope?"

"There was no reason for my parents to stay together after that."

"Yes there was!" Horrified, she looked him straight in the eye, wrapping her hands around his.

"Well, it wasn't enough. They split. Went on with their lives. Left me behind."

"Literally?" She withdrew her hands, indignation rising on his behalf.

"No. Sort of. It's just—I shouldn't complain. I had food on the table. A car to drive once I was old enough."

And yet she could see the layers of pain and the shadows it had left behind.

His hands bunched into fists on the counter like he wanted to lift his hands and bang them down on something to release what he felt inside.

"The conference you were at—Sunshine something? Parents of kids with special needs?" she prompted gently. "Tell me about how that fits into your life. Did they help your sister?"

He shook his head. "They help organize and fund qualified respite care for families when they need a bit of time off. An hour or two here and there."

"They helped your family?"

He shook his head again. "We didn't qualify financially. My parents were both lawyers."

"They're not any longer?"

"My dad quit. Sold off our house and everything in it." There was a bitterness in his tone. "Gave it all to the church and he's now somewhere in Africa doing who knows what."

"When did he go?"

"The day after I graduated high school."

"And your mom?"

"She moved out a few weeks after my sister..." His voice faded and his Adam's apple bobbed as he swallowed hard. "She has a one-bedroom condo. Still works eighty hours a week."

Athena wondered where Chad had gone over Christmas, her heart hurting at the idea that he might have been alone.

"So your family didn't use the Sunshine organization, but you support them?"

"They do good things. They help take care of caregivers so they can do their best." He'd brightened slightly, and she could see that being involved with the organization was a ray of sunshine in his life, a connection of sorts.

"And so that was the photo op? You making a donation?"

"It was only supposed to take five minutes. Me, an over-sized check, a couple of handshakes. A hello-goodbye."

"But then?"

His expression drifted into a memory she'd love to understand.

"You saw someone you knew?" she guessed.

"Yeah." His leg started jiggling, his lower lip dipping under his front teeth. "Some families I hadn't seen in years. We'd go to the socials and support groups together when I was a kid. We got chatting and I lost track of time."

"What were you doing when I came in?" she asked, thinking about the circle, the damp eyes and the calm, soothing tone he'd been using. Understanding, empathy and kindness. An entirely different side of Mr. Chad Mullens compared to his sports-hero image.

"Oh." He scrubbed a hand through his hair, leaving it a mess. "Therapy?" He winced at her.

Adorable. Chadwick Mullens was like a lost, lonely child she wanted to hug and hold, keep safe.

Wait. *Therapy?*

"You're a therapist?"

"No, no." He spread out his hands, his rings shining under the lights above the cash register. "Just a casual group thing. Really, they just share stories. You know, let each other know it's okay to feel the things we feel."

"That's a lot more important than a cookbook photo shoot," she said quietly.

"No. I let you down."

"Chad, what does a cookbook matter compared to easing someone else's pain?"

"You're not mad?"

"How can I be when you're being...you." When he was finally opening up and sharing how he felt. When he was out there helping other people despite his own distress.

He sucked in a deep breath like she'd given him air. Then those blazing eyes of his landed hard on hers and he said with devastating certainty, "Kiss me."

CHAPTER 11

Mullens brushed Athena's lips with his thumb. They were red from kissing, her eyes bright despite her obvious fatigue. She'd been working too hard lately. It was Saturday and she was working. Always working.

Always running.

"Thanks for telling me about your sister and family," she whispered, cuddling into his side and making him feel more at home than he had in several decades.

Earlier, when she'd stepped onto the bottom rung of her stool, lifting herself higher so she could better reach him over the counter during their kiss, he'd slid her across the surface and into his arms. That, it turned out, had been a smart move, as the kiss had gone on for a very long and wonderful time.

He was surprised how light he felt after telling Athena about his sister, his parents, his family. She hadn't looked at him with pity or treated him like a dumb, wounded kid, and that filled him with gratitude.

"I'll try to let you in more."

"Okay."

"But that means you need to let me in as well."

Surprise and indignation flattened her expression. "I do!"

"Yeah? What are *you* running from?"

"I'm not running from anything." She pushed away, clearly insulted, as if he'd touched a sore spot nobody was supposed to notice or acknowledge. She nudged the frames of her glasses higher on her face.

"You're like me."

"Yeah? How's that?" She was facing him now, a challenge held in her posture.

"You find ways to bury the hurt. You keep busy. Obsess over details and rules. Leave no time to think or feel about other things."

"And what makes you think I'm busy?" Her eyes twinkled and she flicked a hand toward the bookshelves to her left.

Hey, fair was fair. If she got to ask direct questions, he did, too.

"You obsess over your subscriber numbers and asked me to go beat up that person who unsubscribed."

"That was a joke!"

He studied her for a long moment, knowing he was on dangerous ground, but that he needed to push if they were going to be real with each other. Truly and scarily real.

"Your mom's in a wheelchair," he stated. "Multiple sclerosis?"

She gave a tiny nod, confirming his guess that Mrs. Gavras had the autoimmune disease, and that it was slowly attacking her nervous system.

"Is she okay?"

Athena's bravado crumpled, her shoulders rounding in, head bowing. His heart raced as he witnessed the sudden change. Tears streaked from under the lenses of her glasses as though someone had turned on a hose, and she started shaking with sobs.

He wrapped his arms around her, rocking her, shocked at the violence of the storm that tore through her. How had she locked all of this inside? There'd been no sign she was struggling so fiercely, other than the odd flicker of what he'd assumed was annoyance or exhaustion.

"Let it all out. I've got you," he whispered.

"You're right," she mumbled once her tears had slowed. "I stay busy because then I don't have to think." Her body trembled in his arms. "Then I don't have to feel."

Boy, did he ever understand that.

"What are you avoiding the most?" He stroked her hair, marveling at its silkiness.

"I see multiple sclerosis stealing my mom and her identity, as well as her vibrancy. I feel guilty whenever I'm not there helping, but she doesn't need me hovering and worrying." Athena nestled her cheek against his chest, then she ducked her head, swiping a sleeve across her face like a tissue. "Will she still be strong enough to hold her grandbabies, assuming I ever find anyone who can put up with me?"

Sobs rocked her again, and Mullens held her through the storm, wanting to be nowhere else but here.

* * *

When Athena believed she'd cried herself close to dehydration, she pulled back from Chad, her eyes a swollen mess. She'd needed that emotional release far more than she'd realized, but now that it was over, she was horribly embarrassed.

"I'm sorry," she whispered, barely able to glance at him. He must think she was a disaster, unable to handle her own life.

And worse—the man had finally opened up about himself, and she'd collapsed in an emotional ball of fatigue, pouring her own pain all over him like he'd declared it open season.

Lonnie had played games, allowing her to think they were connecting when they weren't. But Chad was different. This felt *real*. She'd let him into the deepest, darkest places she kept hidden from others. And he'd talked about things she'd never read about in any of his countless interviews.

She had to believe this was real. That they were trying to move toward something special. She had to trust. Him. Herself. *This*.

She swiped at her wet cheeks, knocking her glasses crooked.

Chad reached out, tenderly lifting the frames from her face. He folded the fabric of his Armadillo Day sweatshirt over the lenses, rubbing them dry one at a time while she wiped her eyes. Athena sniffed, then pulled in a deep breath to center herself.

She reached for her glasses when he re-aimed them at her, but he pulled back, not letting her take them. She lowered her hands and held still while he tenderly placed the frames back on her face. She fought the surge of welling tears. This man had the power to devastate and, despite her abject resistance, had found his way past her armor, rendering her completely vulnerable.

She didn't understand it. She wasn't even sure if she'd forgiven him for the way he gave her so much attitude at work, and here she was kissing him, wanting him, practically ready to keep him.

"You okay?" His head tipped to the side, his quiet calm

making her love him all the more. No wonder those parents had cried on him at that conference. It was like he was a giant magnet, creating a healing current that pulled away a person's pain.

She sniffed and nodded. "Sorry I made it all about me."

"Yeah? How's that?"

"Crying on you. You ask me one little question and *whoosh*." She swept her fingers through the air, mimicking her earlier deluge.

He gave a half shrug. "You opened up. I appreciate the trust."

"And I appreciate yours." She squeezed his arm, hoping he understood just how much she'd needed to hear him share more about himself. "So one other thing…"

"The women?"

The women? Oh, right. The ones always photographed with him. Smiling fans and cheek kisses. She knew that was just for show.

At least she was pretty sure it was.

"Now that you mention it…what's the deal with them? It's never the same one twice."

"I haven't had anything serious in a long time."

"I *know*." She groaned and rolled her eyes, feeling the sudden need to keep her hands busy.

"No, not like that." He followed her to the kitchen, carrying a tray of dirty cups. "Really, Tina. Get your head out of the gutter. The pictures are called 'feeding the social media machine.' Staying relevant and such so I can keep getting deals."

"Would it kill you to call me by my name?"

"Probably." He was so serious she laughed. "Isn't Tina short for Athena?"

"Nobody calls me that."

"Nobody calls me Chad. Or Chadwick."

"Want me to stop?"

"Please don't." His tone was surprisingly tender.

"Okay. I won't." She turned to him. "Out of curiosity, though—why not?"

"I hate the name."

"Oh, lovely," she said drily.

"No, it's okay when you call me that."

"Really? Why?"

"It grounds me. Reminds me who I am."

She blinked at him with a wryness that caused him to shrug helplessly. Adorable.

Seriously. There was no way to stay mad at this man, or even keep a barrier of any sort between him and her stupid softie of a heart.

"Is that why you call me Tina? You think it grounds *me* or keeps me humble?"

His smile was warm. "Maybe. You do have a pretty big ego." There was a playful, wicked glint in his steely eyes.

"You do it because it annoys me!" She batted him with a tea towel, but he grabbed her, tucking her into his arms, holding her so close she couldn't fight him.

It was heaven.

He dropped a light kiss on her lips. "You're the only woman I want, Tina."

"Who's Tina?" Athena frowned as though upset, and to show his remorse, or maybe to make it clear who he meant, he gave her another kiss that wiped her brain clear of any argument she'd been meaning to start.

"It's you," he murmured, his lips trailing a tingling path down the side of her neck. "Always you."

* * *

Mullens didn't want to leave Athena; didn't want to go home and have this evening end.

He was stretched out in an armchair in the middle of her shop, with her in his lap and her arms around his neck. And the kisses. The kisses were pretty amazing.

No, scratch that. Beyond amazing. It was as though everything before Athena had been nothing more than a distraction, a lie. This was the real game. The big leagues.

The real thing.

There was no turning back from Athena Gavras.

She was smart, sexy, curvy, and had one heck of a mouth—both in the way she called him out on his crap as well as in the way she kissed. She was part demanding, part tease. Keeping him guessing and always on his toes.

He never wanted to kiss anyone else ever again.

Never wanted to stop.

Something nudged his calf, and he shook his leg, jostling Athena.

"Am I too heavy?" She pulled away, and he tugged her right back, kissing her again.

But it did feel as though something was trying to climb his leg.

The puppy.

It had the worst timing ever.

He broke the kiss and reached down to scoop up the dog, depositing it in Athena's lap. "I think I may have accidentally adopted this guy."

"So weird," she mused, her lips a ruby red from all that kissing. Irresistible.

He leaned closer, kissing her again until the dog yipped at

them.

"Know where that Brant guy might be? Dylan thinks I adopted this pup, but I thought I was just holding him for a bit."

Mullens rubbed the dog's ears. It unsteadily circled Athena's lap twice before curling up. Athena stared at the dog, then at Mullens for a long moment.

"What?"

She shook her head. "Nothing."

"Tell me? Did I get punked or scammed or something?"

"No, it's just that Brant doesn't give a dog to just anyone. Even if it's ugly."

He covered the pup's ears and shot her a look. "Like your big-headed cat is much better."

"Hey!" She choked on a laugh, the cheery mood a good look on her.

"So this Brant guy?" he pressed. "He's the local vet and animal control officer who takes in rescues...and then just leaves them with people?"

"Usually he's really careful and particular." Athena had that odd look again.

"I make a good impression," he said with a cheesy grin. Immediately he recalled her first impression of him and internally winced, amending his claim. "Usually."

"Do you even want a dog?"

"I don't know." He pulled her in, close enough to kiss. "But I know that I want you."

She tried to hide that smile he loved so much. "We're not talking about me."

"But I'd like to be talking about you. You and me, to be specific."

"Yeah?" she said, her tone full of doubt. "Trying to avoid discussing your future?"

"I thought I was?"

Suddenly she was way too focused on the dog in her lap, and he wondered if she believed that he'd told her a lie earlier: that when it came to women, it was always her.

She was the one he thought about when he woke up, when he cooked or ate. When he worked out or chose an outfit for the day. It was her. Always her.

"Is there a you and me?"

He caught the glint of fear in her eyes and she looked about ready to flee if he gave the wrong answer.

"There sure is. I've even been asking about rentals in town. Landon gave me some stuff that was horribly out of date, but I was—"

"I'm sorry. What?"

"A place for me to stay here in Sweetheart Creek. So we can hang out more without me imposing."

"Imposing?" She slid off his lap and deposited the dog in his arms, laughing. "Chad, I'm not... We're..." She let out a huff of disbelief.

"Too fast?" he asked weakly.

"Yeah."

"Well, I've kind of been crushing on you for a long time. I've been trying to ignore the way you make my heart race, and how stupid things come out of my mouth just so I can stand there having a conversation with you."

Her brow furrowed.

"What?" he asked, feeling a stirring of alarm. "What are you thinking?"

Her eyes were filled with unanswered questions, ones he wished she'd ask. Worries he wished he could lay to rest.

If she wanted to know why he'd been such a jerk the first time they'd met, he'd tell her. He'd give her blood, tears, sweat and confessions.

He steadied himself, knowing he had to be honest, not change the subject or pass it off as a joke. He might get only one shot at this.

"You suck the air from rooms," she said quickly.

He blinked, trying to sort out her words and what they meant. Was sucking the air from rooms a bad thing?

"You have this way of sweeping in with your hypnotizing charm, and everyone just stops thinking and falls at your feet."

He started, surprised at how wounded she sounded.

She leaned over him, hands on the chair's armrests, her body intoxicatingly close. "How do I know this is real?"

He forced himself to look up from her curves, to stop imagining what it would take to have her lips back on his, making his fantasies come true. "What does your heart tell you?"

"It tells me to be scared."

CHAPTER 12

onnie gestured for Athena to wait for him off to one side of the arena hallway. When he'd texted her to meet up before his team played the Dragons, she'd said sure. But when she'd asked him what it was about, he'd ghosted her.

Now they were here, face-to-face, with his team filtering past. Athena smiled and said hello to some of the familiar faces. Davenport, Lonnie's friend and usual roomie when on the road, enveloped her in an enthusiastic hug, lifting her from her feet.

She laughed as he set her back down. "Don't let the Dragons see you doing that or they'll think I've switched teams on them."

"And why wouldn't you? We're going to slay tonight." He pretended to swing a sword through the air. "Hey, what have you been up to? You're looking even hotter than usual. Seeing anyone?"

"Actually…" Was she? Were she and Chad an official thing? If so, she wanted to move slowly and be sure this time. No being swept into a romance at high speed and then smack straight into reality like she had with Lonnie.

Her ex pushed Davenport out of the way. "We've gotta chat. Skedaddle, man."

Davenport held out a fist for Athena to bump as he stepped backward, away from them. "Don't let this loser convince you to take him back. There are better fish in the sea." He winked again and hustled away as Lonnie pretended to go after him.

Athena sighed as Lonnie continued to act as if he was going to fight Davenport. Her family had seen through his charm, but she'd been so dazzled she'd lost her normal twenty-twenty vision where he was concerned. The man had some serious gravitational pull. The very idea of someone semifamous choosing her had swept away her rationality, making her believe she was different. That she was special.

Chad had a similar gravitational pull, and she felt a flash of panic. What if his interest wasn't genuine? What if he saw her as nothing more than a challenge—could he lure the serious, rule-following team dietician into his arms?

She shook her head. Chad wasn't like that. He had a tender side, a side so human and vulnerable she knew he was different from Lonnie, despite her fears otherwise.

"What's up?" she asked impatiently, as Lonnie waited for his teammates to finish trickling past.

His expression was tender, that same one that had made her feel like she was part of his inner circle. The look, she now knew, was one he used on almost everyone.

She crossed her arms.

"I had to put Banx down."

"What?" Athena felt as though someone had knocked the

wind out of her. She hadn't even known his cat, Banx the Manx, was sick. "Why didn't you tell me?"

"I just did."

"But before?"

"Because he's my cat?"

"It was like he was mine. For a bit."

"Until you ditched over that stupid thing with Lauren."

"It was *not* stupid. And I cared about Banxie, okay?"

"What were you gonna do? Fly out and see him? It's a cat."

"Maybe I would have," she said.

"You're busy."

"How would you know?"

"You always are. Especially when you're upset."

"I'm not upset."

He gave her a smug, knowing smile. "Babe…"

"Keeping busy is how I deal with things."

She'd started her first cookbook when her mom had needed to use a cane more often and Athena wasn't still in Texas to help, then had ramped up the project when she'd begun to suspect Lonnie wasn't as committed to their relationship as she was. Now she was on book two, the project she'd pitched her publisher a week after her dad had bought her mom a wheelchair. And to distract herself from her frustration and her inappropriate crush on Chad last fall, she'd said yes to opening a store with Meddy.

None of that meant she was upset. She just had a lot to deal with, and being busy was a productive way to channel that potential anxiety.

"I'm late," she said, angling away. "Meddy's waiting."

"How is feisty Maddy?"

"*Meddy.*" She was never sure if Lonnie was truly incapable

of remembering her sister's name, or if he just enjoyed acting as though she mattered so little he couldn't be bothered.

He rolled his eyes at her correction, immediately bringing back the futile anger from a thousand fights and the dismissive way he'd treated her when she'd confronted him about the woman he was seeing on the side.

"I hope you lose tonight," she muttered, spinning away to storm down the hallway. She swiped at her eyes, furious at herself for letting him get under her skin.

Or maybe it was the loss of Banx hitting her. The feline had been a good friend during the short time they'd shared Lonnie's condo. They'd spent many hours waiting for him to come home, and she hadn't felt as lonely with her furry little pal curled up beside her.

She reached the end of the hall and came to a stop, realizing someone was blocking her way. Tall, wide and looking ready to maim.

The man was fully decked out in one of his retro-cut suits, his fingers covered in rings, his hair a sexy and unruly bedhead mess.

Her boyfriend. The idea made her stomach quiver, then drop out like it had gone over a cliff without her body.

"Aren't you supposed to be getting dressed?" Athena asked Chad, attempting to push past him.

His hands locked around her biceps. "Why are you crying?" His deep voice was lower than usual, and the surrounding air bristled with masculine energy.

She lifted her hands and swiped at her damp cheeks. "I'm not."

"Fine. Tears of joy. Where've you been all week?"

"Busy. We're at over eight thousand subscribers, and my publisher asked me to write some articles."

He held her gaze for a long moment, and she knew he intuited the truth—that she'd been avoiding him a teensy bit. She felt it was the only way to slow their relationship pace, because with Chad, she sensed there was only one speed —supersonic.

They'd shared a few tender secrets as well as amazing kisses, and she knew how easy it would be to ignore her doubts and jump in with both feet. They needed to form a strong foundation of trust over time, otherwise their relationship wouldn't be able to withstand the problems thrown at them, and everything would shake and crumble apart.

"I miss you." He pulled her in for a long, deep kiss, leaving her breathless when he released her.

"I miss you, too." She pressed lightly against his chest, forcing herself to slide from his arms. "Go get ready for your game."

He caught her hand, his eyes cutting over her shoulder in the direction she'd come from. "Don't judge all of us based on him."

"Chad…"

"I get that you're scared, and that he hurt you."

She met his eyes, almost expecting to see her fears returned. Instead, she saw something scarier.

She looked away, wishing she had the courage to feel all the things he did. To trust in them, and for that trust to be enough.

"That guy and I are nothing alike. Nothing, Tina."

"What's the difference?" She focused on him, desperately hoping he'd produce a nice little chart illustrating what she could trust and believe. Something concrete so her heart could finally overrule her terrified mind and she could just…

let go. Let go and not care if one of them hit the supersonic button.

"Everything," he said. "Absolutely everything that matters. And I will fight through your fears until you're able to see it."

* * *

"What on earth has gotten into Mullens?" Cassandra McTavish asked, leaning forward to get a better view of the ice. She was dating the team's goalie and had been to a few games lately with Hannah and Jenny, but instead of sitting in the usual VIP sky box tonight, Cass, Jenny, Meddy and Athena were down by center ice. In fact, Meddy had insisted Cass hire a babysitter for her son and Landon's daughter so the gals could have a proper girls night out.

As one, Meddy and Jenny echoed Cass's posture, craning their necks to follow the players.

Athena ignored them, her mind still out in the hallway, processing Lonnie's words. If she did get busy when she was upset, then why was she still running so hard? Last year, keeping busy had prevented her from thinking about how often Lonnie was away, about how far she was from her family and about her mom's health. Plus it had been productive. She'd come out of it with a cookbook, a second one in the works, as well as a job with a professional sports team. Much better than sitting at home worrying.

But now her life was even more hectic, when by all accounts it was good. She was close to home again, spending time with her family, and she had great jobs and friendships, as well as a hunky new boyfriend.

There was nothing to be upset about. She should be letting loose, going to her monthly book club meetings and curling up in Chad's home library several nights a week. Shouldn't she?

Maybe staying busy was about more than her just being upset. Maybe she also used it to avoid thinking about scary things, such as the idea that Chad might be serious about proving how different he was than Lonnie.

What if Chad was The One?

She'd already fallen for him. She'd studiously tried to deny that truth, but she'd seen the photos of herself for the new cookbook cover. The rescheduled photo shoot had finally occurred, and Chad had been amazing, practically making love to the camera. And his effect had haloed, making her a glowing, beautiful, bright-eyed happy woman.

She knew it wasn't just the makeup and lights, because in the first photo shoot she hadn't glowed. Not even slightly.

Despite pumping the brakes, she was in love.

Athena let out a shuddery breath, letting the scary truth settle into her bones. She clenched her hands into fists, resisting the urge to get up and do something in order to distract herself.

A player from the other team slammed into the boards in front of her and she jumped as his helmet hit the Plexiglass with a clack. Lonnie's exposed cheek pressed against the translucent barrier before he slid down and out of sight.

The Dragon who'd body-checked her ex looked up with burning rage firing his eyes. As he met Athena's gaze the anger melted into something softer, something that took her breath away.

She blinked, and Chad was gone.

"Was that Lonnie again?" Meddy asked, frowning at the player currently shaking off a hit while slowly skating back into position.

"Sure was," Jenny confirmed.

"Mullens has been hitting him hard tonight," Meddy said casually, making it clear she thought something was up between the two men.

"I haven't seen this much fight in the team all season," Jenny said, slurping on her tall drink of sweet tea. Her eyes cut toward the newly returned-to-play center, Dylan, as he glided onto the ice as though his ankle injury had never happened.

Fight was the right word. Athena wanted to scold Chad for being such a hotheaded goon. Either that or wrap her legs around him and kiss him hard for being protective or romantic or whatever he was trying to be. Because she knew these fights were for her. For the tears Lonnie had caused her to shed, and the fears he'd planted in her heart.

"Anyone need more popcorn?" she asked, feeling antsy. "Drinks? Hot dogs?"

"Sit." Her sister grabbed her arm, holding her down. "You've already hit the concession twice."

"Are you and Mullens finally dating?" Jenny asked. The group of women scanned the ice, searching for him.

At that moment, as though conjured, Chad skated past. He looked up, his eyes connecting with Athena's and she felt the heat of their earlier kiss. He lifted a glove, pointing a finger at her while skating backward, eyes still on her, his slow smile warming her heart.

He would protect her. He had her back.

Man, he was sexy.

"You and Mullens?" Meddy cackled. "About freaking time."

"Wait, though." Jenny frowned. "Didn't you call all hockey players heartbreakers?"

"They are," she said breathlessly, unable to look away.

Her sister gasped as she spun to face Athena, clutching her arm. "He's beating him up for you!"

"Who?" Cass asked, her eyes flitting over the ice in confusion.

"Nobody," Athena told her.

"Didn't you talk to Lonnie earlier?" Meddy demanded.

Athena kept her gaze lowered and focused on drinking her sweet tea.

"Something happened."

"*Nothing* happened."

"Tell me."

Athena sighed and dropped her shoulders in defeat, knowing her sister wouldn't let up until she had the truth. She whispered, "Chad saw me crying."

Meddy gasped, half standing, her voice loud and clear. "Lonnie made you cry?" She immediately scanned the ice as though she planned to jump the barriers and fight Lonnie as well.

"No! Not like that. Sit." She grabbed her sister. "I'm just tired and was feeling frustrated. And Banxie died."

Meddy gave her a look filled with such sympathy a lump formed in Athena's throat. Slinging an arm over her shoulders, her sister pulled her in for a quick half hug.

"I'm fine," Athena said. "Really."

Meddy's eyes narrowed as though she was reading a truth meter. "And Mullens saw you crying."

"Yes."

"And now he's being all protective." Her lips curved up in a smile. "That's really sexy, you know."

Jenny nodded.

"It's dysfunctional," Athena stated, though her tone lacked

conviction. There was no way she'd admit how sexy she found the fighting.

"Who?" Cass complained, clearly impatient about being left out.

"Mullens and Lonnie," Meddy explained.

"Who's Lonnie?"

"Athena's ex on the other team." Meddy tapped her cup against Athena's. "Admit it. It's hot."

"Super hot," Cass said with a grin, having caught up with what was happening between the men.

"Someone's getting lucky tonight," Jenny predicted in a singsongy tone. "Get him to kiss you on the inside of your elbow. Totally erogenous."

"You need help," Cass muttered, shooting her a sly smile.

Jenny crowed, "You tried it! It was sexy! Admit it!"

Cass shrugged, her cheeks turning pink.

"What are they talking about?" Meddy asked.

"No clue." Athena sagged in her seat, scrunched her eyes shut and rubbed the heels of her hands into her forehead, trying to relieve the growing tension.

Chad and his behavior were hot, sexy *and* dysfunctional.

She really, really wanted to enjoy this. To leap into his arms, wrap her legs around his waist and kiss him silly. But the idea of him fighting her battles—in a war that had already ended—felt...

She didn't even know how it felt. She'd never had a boyfriend act like this before and she couldn't decide if it was super sexy or frustratingly antiquated. Did he believe she couldn't take care of her own business?

"It's sweet," her sister said, nudging her.

"Yeah, he's telling you he loves you in Neanderthal," Jenny said, slurping on her drink.

The other women burst into laughter.

"He doesn't *love* me," Athena muttered, knowing her face had turned red. "And remind me to loan you my favorite new caveman romance."

Jenny grimaced. "That's a thing?"

She nodded knowingly.

"Mullens *likes* you," her sister sang, then sighed dreamily. "He's expressing his truest feelings."

"With his fists," Athena argued.

"He's a man, Athena. An alpha who's feeling protective. And he's smart. He's using the bounds of the game to beat up your ex and send him a message."

"Except Lonnie and I are so totally over."

"Then maybe that message is for you."

* * *

Mullens exited the locker room, hoisting his bag over his shoulder. He looked left on instinct and felt the lift of a smile.

There was his woman.

She saw him, her face turning red, her gaze darting away as though shy. Her right arm crossed over her chest as she toyed with her necklace, her left arm across her middle. She licked her top lip and came closer, as though unsure what sort of reception she might receive, uncertain what she could expect from him and their relationship.

He wanted her to expect the best. To expect everything she'd ever wanted and to know that she'd never be denied.

"Hey." He bent, placing a light kiss on her lips.

"What was that out there?" she asked. Her gaze kept darting up to his, then away.

"A pretty good game, wouldn't you say?" he replied, grinning.

"More penalties than usual," she pointed out.

"Yeah." He'd been a bit rougher. And for good reason. He locked his eyes on Athena.

"Tina," he said, pressing her closer to the wall, blocking out the surrounding men who were whooping it up over their win as they made their way out of the locker room. "You and me? We're a team. Someone makes you cry, I take care of it."

She stared at him for a long moment.

"Defend the net like it's something that matters to you," Coach had told him.

No problem. All he'd had to do was think of Athena.

"Do you think Lonnie made me cry?"

"Yeah. Because he did."

That man had hurt her, caused her to feel as if she didn't matter. He'd made her feel small.

And a woman like Athena should soar.

She should be able to trust her heart.

Mullens wanted the time back that she'd wasted on Lonnie. He wanted to deliver it to her. Mend her.

And he couldn't do that. But he was a forward for the Dragons, and he could attack. Attack the other team so they couldn't go after his own. He could go after the man who'd made her so afraid to give her heart to another.

"I was crying earlier because our cat died," Athena said.

Our. Our cat.

He clenched his jaw. Lonnie didn't deserve to be a part of anything with her. Now or ever.

But he also knew there was something more than a beloved animal passing away that had caused those tears. He'd seen it written across her face. The frustration, the hurt, the anger.

"Well," he said gently, "after tonight, he won't let one of his pets die ever again."

She laughed, delight brightening her eyes, and Mullens realized Athena Gavras might find him and his possibly possessive aggression sexy after all.

"You okay with me getting a little rough?" He winced dramatically, trying for cute.

"A *little*?" She huffed a laugh, leaning into him.

"A lot?" Mullens savored the feeling of her body pressed against his. It felt like forgiveness and divine possibility. "He deserved every bit of it."

"Yeah?" Her arms were snaking upward, her palms tracing a path up his chest. He snugged her closer.

"Yeah. Anyone who hurts my Tina has to answer to me."

"Well, there was this one time in fourth grade when Cole Wylder accidentally knocked me down on the playground and I broke my retainer."

"You want me to go after him?"

She nodded, eyes wide, playing up her role. Darn if she wasn't the cutest thing he'd ever seen.

"Tell me where he lives," he growled.

She laughed again, her face awash with joy.

Man, he loved this woman.

* * *

"I need you to get Mullens on board."

Athena looked up from her monitor, where she'd been watching a clip of Chad talking to a reporter. As he chatted, a woman came up, flipping up the hem of her shirt to reveal her tanned, hard midriff. Without missing a beat, Chad had accepted the marker she'd offered and scrawled his name across her stomach as though claiming ownership.

Athena knew this was part of his image, but it made her stomach tighten and roll like it was trying to knot itself. Had the man even considered saying no?

Maybe he enjoyed it. She poked at her own belly through her silk blouse, unimpressed with the way it swallowed her finger.

Some dietician she was.

But it wasn't just the female fans with lithe bodies throwing themselves at him. That came with the territory, along with the clips they ran of him smiling in selfies with different women, letting the audience believe he'd dated them all. No, it was the following gala clip that had caused her head to start pounding. In the clip he'd been looking handsome, a glass of whiskey in hand, his fitted suit exuding power, his smile filled with devilish charm. He'd been commanding the row of men behind him, also with drinks at the ready.

In the interview, Chad and the reporter had been talking about the upcoming cookbook, and a small square had popped up in the corner of the screen, revealing him on its cover. Meanwhile, the drinks clips rolled in the other corner, negating everything he said about diet and taking care of one's body.

The dull throbbing in Athena's temples had increased.

She could argue that the photos and clips were taken out of context, but she'd been there. He'd spilled that apple-infused drink on her. She'd been sticky with it and had tasted its sweetness.

She thought about flipping over to her online cooking

channel, but didn't want to see how far her number of subscribers had plummeted thanks to this dietary scandal.

She choked on a laugh. Dietary scandal. Boy, she sure knew how to do sexy, didn't she? What did Chad even see in her beyond the challenge?

"Athena?" Coach Louis was still standing in her doorway and she jolted, having completely fallen into her own thoughts about Chad. "We need Mullens on board," he repeated.

"Right." They'd talked about this before.

"Have you seen the footage from last month's gala?" Louis stepped into her office, his sneakers silent on the carpet. "I've put Nuvella on it and I have a call in with his agent. For now, we're planning to lie low and let it blow over, but this could get really nasty on us. Overpaid alcoholics on ice, you know?"

Athena pushed back from her desk and nodded. This current angle could give the team a bit of a black eye, plus tank her cookbook's pre-order sales, or even have it pulled from publication before it hit the shelves in March. She'd never get a book deal again.

"I believe Chad's actually on board," she said tentatively, expecting an argument.

"That's what he tells me." He took the chair opposite her desk.

"Well," Athena said carefully, "how's his performance on the ice?"

"He's all over the place." After a short pause, Louis asked, "Are the two of you dating?"

"I'm sorry?" She blinked, her thoughts spiraling into what-if scenarios. Was she supposed to have told human resources they were sort-of-dating?

Maybe they already were. They kissed like they were. They'd shared a few intimate secrets like they were.

And yet they were both so busy they hadn't even been on what she'd consider an official date.

"You dated Lonnie from Jersey Storm?" Louis asked. Her face must've registered surprise because he leaned back, lifting his hands in the air as though needing to defend himself. "I'm sorry. I know that's personal. I'm just trying to get to the bottom of his behavior. You know, look at the whole enchilada where Mullens is concerned."

"And that is a mighty big enchilada."

He chuckled.

"And yeah, Lonnie and I dated. And Chad and I are..." She sighed, suddenly embarrassed. From Louis's point of view, her dating the player who gave her the most amount of grief probably appeared as a lapse in judgment. "I don't know. Interested? Trying? Failing?" She lifted her shoulders in a helpless shrug, hoping she wasn't blushing.

Louis nodded. "I guess that explains why Mullens attacked Lonnie on the ice the other night. He spent a lot of time in the sin bin rather than out there doing what he's good at."

"I'm sorry, I think he believed he was helping me."

"Got it," Louis said. He leaned forward, hands on his knees as if he planned to stand. He paused. "Can you confirm he follows your diet plan?"

"Yes."

Louis settled back in the chair. "So why's he a jerk to you?"

Athena lowered her head, embarrassed by how she'd let herself be used as a prop to enforce Chad's reputation. His rule-breaking illusion was like a magician's sleight of hand, making you think you saw something, when in fact your brain was simply making assumptions and erroneous cognitive leaps based on what he'd already established—his reputation. She'd been an unwilling part of the magic trick, and didn't know how to convince anyone that it wasn't anything more.

"The team needs to respect you, and they're taking leadership cues from him. You're great at what you do, but..." Louis was positioning to stand again. Athena felt a stirring of panic.

But was never a good word, and she was failing the team. She was the easiest person to fire. That would really decimate her own currently declining reputation.

"I'm still digging into why he takes such exception to me and my diet plans," she said quickly. "But I can confirm that in private he follows them and uses my recipes. He's serious about his career."

Louis nodded, thinking that over. He stood. "I'm going to check in again—say, at the end of February? Give you about a month? In the meantime, you know where to find me. We've got to get this guy straightened out and the team on board."

Athena stood as well. "Yes, of course." She followed him to the door, then closed it behind him. She let out a long sigh, sagging in defeat.

What woman in her right mind would date a man who was in the process of possibly destroying two of her careers? Chad might be different from Lonnie, but he still had the ability to cause significant damage.

She wasn't just going to lose her heart with this one. She was going to lose everything.

And the more she thought about it, the worse it seemed. His flagrant flouting of her diet rules and plans, his dependence on charm instead of consistent effort, his belief that a few shared childhood wounds were a strong enough foundation for them to trust each other...

She was never going to learn, was she?

New player, new lessons.

But the lessons all led to the same result—a broken heart.

* * *

Mullens caught up with Athena near the arena's employee exit. She was heading to the private parking lot in the back, no doubt ready to go home. He fell into step beside her.

Louis had pulled him aside over the gala clip of him and the men drinking. He couldn't speak for the other guys, but he'd personally been enjoying some watered-down apple juice that he'd intended to pass for whiskey.

He was pretty sure Louis hadn't believed him about the juice. Like everyone else, he saw what Mullens had wanted: that rules didn't apply here.

Coach was mad.

Athena as well, if her marching pace and the grim lines bracketing her luscious mouth were anything to go on. He'd kind of been hoping she'd laugh at his situation and call him a silly fool for creating such an awful persona in the first place. He'd also been hoping for another one of those kisses that branded his soul.

Which was dumb. Her cookbook could be on the line. And she'd probably gotten an earful from Louis. All because of him.

But everyone would get over it, right?

"Attention equals money," he said. "And money equals happy managers and executives." He'd bet Athena would soon be looking at a raise and a third cookbook contract once this all blew over.

Hopefully.

"And at what cost?"

Okay, so right now it probably looked like he'd sent an exploding torpedo her way. She wasn't used to having her integrity and professional image under fire the way that he was. She had a right to be upset.

"Truth? The last drink I had was a beer during my summer break, before camp started."

She let out a snort of disbelief.

"I wouldn't lie to you," he said, matching her stride.

She turned, eyes ablaze. "Louis is looking to make cuts."

Mullens stopped as though he'd slammed into something. He'd built his personal financial wealth on the strength of his image. Could it all go terribly wrong on him? Could it not only crash his career, get him kicked off this last-chance team, but also get him punted into the next county by the woman who'd captured his heart?

If there was ever a time to follow his dad's lead and join the church, it was probably now. Although he didn't think God would appreciate him coming to him in prayer now that his life was in shambles. Where had he been during the good times? Not in a church.

"You saw the gala clip?" he asked, knowing she had. Her face turned red, and she stopped to face him. "You okay?"

"Well, I'm about to get fired and possibly lose my new cookbook." With a curt nod she resumed marching toward the exit. "Other than that, I'm just peachy!" She slammed the metal door's long handle, blasting the heavy door open like it was made of cardboard.

Okay, this was way worse than he'd assumed. This wasn't just a hammer coming down on him and rippling out to her. She was the one taking the full hit.

He glanced back at the arena, resolving to focus on one problem at a time, to start at the beginning.

"Louis?" he confirmed, falling into step beside her again, the Texas evening sun warm on his skin.

"Yeah. Thanks for standing up for me, by the way." She unlocked her car and slid into the driver's seat.

He grabbed the door. "I told him you're doing your job, that I'm following the plan and that this is all on me."

"Exactly." She looked up at him with so much hurt in her eyes that he released the door.

"I'll fix this. All of it. I promise."

"Good." She slammed it shut and left the parking lot with a squeal of tires.

He had to fix…everything. He just had no idea what all that included or where to start.

CHAPTER 13

Athena dragged herself up the front steps of her parents' wide front porch, balancing the platter of leftover huckleberry tarts her sister had forgotten to take from the shop. She opened the screen door and it hissed, feeling different. She looked down at its hinges, noticing white hydraulic tubes. She released the door. It stayed open.

She smiled. Meddy had found a contractor.

Athena reached to open the inner door and as she took a step forward she stumbled. She caught the tray of tarts in the nick of time and looked down. A ramp. A short one, but with enough of a slope that the two-inch rise from the porch to the house was no longer a problem for a wheelchair.

She'd have to remind Meddy to tell her what her half cost. Weird that her sister hadn't mentioned it already. Although maybe she had, and Athena had dropped it from her fully-crammed mind.

She needed to slow down, breathe, lower her stress. Would it be a big deal if she lost her dietician job or the cookbook contract because of Chad's behavior? Not really. She had the store. And you didn't need much in the way of pride to run your own business in a small town.

She'd just never date again. Ever.

Noticing the screen door was still open, she pushed on it, releasing its latch, noting that there was an expensive sports car parked out front of the neighbor's house a few doors down. Why was it that any nice car made her think of Chad? She needed a brain wash. Something that would erase him from her mind.

The door hissed shut, the new hydraulics slowing its movement. Nice. Now, as her mom came and went on her own with her cane or wheelchair, it wouldn't bang into her.

"Hello?" she called. The fatigue and general glumness that had been following her since she'd snapped at Chad for the gala clip slid away as she took in the familiar living room. She had a lot to be grateful for. From the new ramp that allowed her mother more freedom, to the fact that the store was doing all right, to how her cookbook was a wrap—if it didn't get canceled despite the rumor that its pre-order numbers were up thanks to Chad's mini scandal. And tonight she got to enjoy breakfast and games with her family. She was no longer living afar, like she had been last year while in Jersey with Lonnie.

She wasn't even going to think about Chad tonight.

Not about how much she missed him, or how much it hurt that his professional image was about to destroy her own. Or how the media storm surrounding him and her cookbook had suddenly calmed. It was like she was in the eye of the hurricane, fearing the next round was just about to hit.

She'd literally been locking herself in her arena office, knowing she had to avoid Chad. If she didn't, her stupid seahorse ovaries might decide to wave off their very real relationship problems and forgive him. There was just too much in need of fixing. She'd kidded herself into believing it would all be okay, ignoring the red flags that surrounded getting involved with him.

And she definitely wasn't going to think about how much she wished they'd found a way to make a relationship work for them. Or how much she longed for another one of those hot kisses that made her feel so wanted and needed. Understood.

She hadn't heard from him since she'd ghosted his first two text messages shortly after she'd marched out of the arena over a week and a half ago, high on her anger and the fear of losing her job and book contract.

Not hearing from him after that stung more than she wanted to admit. A lot more. She'd expected him to at least try, to be relentless.

Instead, it was as if he'd simply moved on, and as though the easy laughter and flirtation while cooking shoulder to shoulder in her videos hadn't been special to him.

She hated cooking now. Well, not quite, but filming videos with other NHLers wasn't in the same galaxy as having Chadwick Mullens behind her counter.

Balancing the tarts, she rounded the short hall that junctioned the living room, bedrooms and kitchen. She stopped short.

A tall man with wonderfully broad shoulders was washing his hands at the kitchen sink. She knew that frame. Knew the way the broad torso narrowed at the hips. The way his dark hair needed a trim.

That hunk was the reason for her broken heart.

Why was she such a hopeless fool when it came to men

like Chad? She'd known. *Known*. And she'd gone ahead and fallen, anyway.

"Hey, Athena," Meddy said, taking the platter from her. "Thanks for bringing these."

"What's he doing here?" She dragged her sister to the kitchen doorway. Meddy, who had been setting the tarts on the island counter, stumbled and flailed as Athena manhandled her into the living room before Chad could turn around to check out the clattering behind him.

"He made the ramps and worked on the screen door," Meddy whispered, her eyes wide.

"He's not a contractor."

"Even better, because he didn't charge. And you should see Mom. She's grinning like crazy."

"You asked him?"

Meddy smiled, but before Athena could get upset with her sister, Chad appeared in the living room doorway.

"What do you know about construction?" Athena demanded, hands on her hips.

His Adam's apple bobbed. "A bit, I guess." He shot Meddy an apologetic grimace. " I should head out."

"Were you helping out at Maverick's?" Athena asked, needing to know how he'd ended up here, in her town, working on her family's home. Had he driven out with other Dragons to work on the team captain's farmhouse? Or were he and Meddy in cahoots?

"He gave me some scrap bits of plywood for the ramps, but I'm not really part of the gang over there."

"Then what part are you?"

He shrugged, looking like the loner kid on the playground. Damn, but that pulled on her heartstrings.

His perfect wool sweater had sawdust clinging to it,

suggesting he'd been roped into this somehow, that he hadn't come prepared to work construction on the Gavras home.

"Mav would say yes if you asked," Athena said, giving in a little.

"Yeah, but I may never get out of there again," Chad joked.

"True." The house, from what she'd heard, was an endless pit of renovations.

Her parents came down the hallway from their bedroom, Darianna in the lead. Her face lit up as she spun her wheelchair their way. "Did somebody call me? I felt my ears burning."

"Hey, Mom," Athena said, bending to kiss her on the cheek.

"I should go," Chad said again, hesitantly enough that it was clear he was hoping someone would stop him.

"Excuse me, Chad, but this has already been discussed." Darianna was using her Mom tone and Athena cringed. "You're staying for supper."

"I have a pretty strict diet." His eyes cut to Athena.

"This is one of Athena's recipes, so you should be fine."

"It's not like you follow the diet anyway," she muttered. She instantly wished she could take back her words, knowing they weren't true, and that it was an unfair dig.

It didn't help that he seemed less larger-than-life than usual today. More humble and subdued, like a kid afraid he was going to be kicked out.

But she had a right to her anger. It was him lying about his diet that had put two of her careers on the rocks.

"Actually," Athena said, feeling a sudden lightness as she thought of the perfect excuse to have him leave, "Chadwick doesn't do pancakes. And tonight is breakfast and games."

His mouth dropped open and his eyes cast downward,

hiding the flash of pain that had crossed them like lightning through a night sky.

"Chad, hon," Darianna said, shooting Athena a look of disappointment, "you are always welcome here. And you don't have to eat pancakes. We're serving other things as well. We'll put on extra scrambled eggs and whole grain toast, won't we, Athena? Do you like eggs?"

He nodded and everyone was silent for a beat, Athena feeling put in her place for being rude and unwelcoming.

"And actually," he said quietly, "I do eat pancakes. I just haven't in a long time."

"Well, if you want them, we have them. If you don't, no harm done. Now let's get this show on the road. Everyone must be hungry." Darianna wheeled into the kitchen, taking charge. Meddy set the table while Neandro began piling ingredients on the counter. Chad went to the back door off the kitchen and let his little dog in from the fenced yard.

"He's such a sweet boy," her mom said, referring to the hulking, strong man. She lifted her voice and patted her lap, cooing at the puppy, "Come here, you little ragamuffin."

The dog was across the room in a few bounds, landing on her lap and curling into a ball as if he'd done it all his life.

What on earth had gone on here today?

"You adopted it?" Athena asked Chad.

"*It* has a name," he said pointedly, obviously feeling enough at home to poke at her.

"Stitches," Meddy said.

"You named him Stitches?"

"Nah, Brant did. It kind of works, don't you think?"

Athena shrugged.

"What can I do to help, Mrs. Gavras?" Chad asked, standing beside her wheelchair.

With a smile, she rolled backward. "Call me Darianna. You good with a knife?"

"Not especially, but he still has all of his digits," Athena muttered.

Chad wiggled his fingers to prove it.

"Good enough for this kitchen. Make the fruit salad, dear." Her mom gestured to the fruit bowl in the middle of the counter, giving Athena a warning glance, before turning warmly to the hockey player. "Whatever you want in the salad, chop up and put in the big bowl. Athena, you make the eggs," she added. "And Neandro, did you start the sausage?"

He tilted the sizzling pan in his wife's direction.

"Don't drop them!" She laughed, and he quickly swung the pan, tipping the rolling turkey sausages back to safety.

Chad smiled, seeming comfortably ensconced in her family's kitchen. What. On. Earth?

It was going to be difficult staying upset with a man who fit here. A man who was at home in the heart of everything that mattered to her.

* * *

Mullens knew he was pushing it with Athena by staying for supper. Not replying to his texts last week had sent a pretty clear message, as had her little conversational digs in front of her family. She wanted him to go away and stay away.

But there was no way he could pry himself out of this kitchen, even though, for her sake, he probably should. It was like a hook had been sunk in deep, anchoring him here.

He'd missed joking around in the kitchen and being part of a family.

Athena's parents were so warm and welcoming that he

could see why she was such an amazing woman. She had their warmth and smarts, their humor and sense of fun.

And yet right now Athena wasn't having fun. He'd been working behind the scenes to make things right in her life again, and while he was beyond deserving forgiveness, there was still a flicker of hope burning inside him. Or maybe it was stupidity. Either way, it spurred him onward in his quest to continue fixing all the things he'd mishandled.

"You may have heard that your daughter and I got off on the wrong foot," he said tentatively, breaking a momentary lapse in the chatter.

Athena, who was finishing up the eggs, turned from the stove, blinking at him. She looked hurt, almost as if she was going to cry. Or maybe scream.

"I did hear something," Mrs. Gavras admitted.

"What happened?" Meddy asked, giving Athena a cautious glance, as though aware she was treading where a younger sister might not be welcome.

"It wasn't her fault."

Athena had turned back to the stove and hunched her shoulders, like she wanted to block out his words.

"She said something that reminded me of my sister. Evonne." Mullens focused on slicing the rind away from the sweet center of a honeydew melon, not on the way it hurt saying his sister's name out loud. It was like breaking through the thin ice on top of a puddle, the frigid water below zipping straight to his nerve endings, making them zing.

"You hated her?" Meddy asked, her voice rising with surprise.

"Meddy!" Athena snapped, her eyes wide with alarm as she peeked at Mullens.

"No. We were really close, actually. But she passed away when I was thirteen."

He inhaled, then exhaled. As the team's therapist had promised, it was getting easier to talk about. He'd told a lot of people about Evonne recently, working on becoming the kind of man who could open up and be an equal to a woman like Athena.

It still hurt, but he no longer felt the impulse to lash out or shut down.

"Oh, hon." Darianna's eyes filled with sorrow, as though she'd known the girl herself.

"So we got off on the wrong foot because I reminded you of Evonne?" Athena said, moving to his side. She placed her hand over his, gently encouraging him to release the knife handle he'd been squeezing. "Why? What did I do?"

She watched him, her head tipped to one side, and he wondered where they'd be right now if he'd taken care of his grief much sooner. But maybe it wasn't too late, and with some serious effort he could get them there.

"If I could take back that moment," he murmured, "I would."

"Grief is a funny thing," Mrs. Gavras said. "It comes at the most inconvenient times."

"What did I do?" Athena repeated, her expression stricken, as though she was ready to blame herself for the battle they'd been engaged in since day one.

Over the lump in his throat, he managed to say, "Broccoli and pancakes."

* * *

Broccoli and pancakes? Was Chad joking? How on earth had all this conflict between them come from two unassuming foods?

"I used to tell my sister a joke about broccoli," Chad said, as they put the last dishes on the table and took their seats. Athena's mom sat at one end, her father at the other, Meddy across from her. Chad was at Athena's right, having hustled in to take the chair closest to her mom, then lifting his dog from Darianna's lap to set him on the floor. Both Darianna and Stitches had given him a sad look.

Meddy groaned. "Not that stupid joke Athena tells?"

He nodded slowly.

"What's the difference between broccoli and boogers?" Athena confirmed.

"Kids won't eat broccoli!" her dad crowed, scooping fruit salad onto his plate.

Chad smiled weakly.

Athena's heart sank. One moment of goofing around and she'd been inadvertently insensitive, sinking their potential relationship before it was even out of the harbor.

"New-player orientation," she whispered. She'd assumed her immaturity had turned him off. She hadn't even considered the joke had been a trigger of some sort. But why would she? Who had a trigger involving booger jokes?

"And what about the pancakes?" Meddy asked, wading into the conversation as though she'd never felt pain a day in her life and didn't understand the mine field she was dancing through. She waved the plate of carrot cake pancakes at him.

He hesitated, his face pale, then slowly took it and served himself one.

Athena watched, speechless.

"Your sister liked pancakes?" Darianna asked.

Chad nodded. "A lot. Last thing we ate as a family before she…" His eyes were desperate and he frantically waved the serving dish about, finding nowhere near him to set it down.

Athena snatched it from him and he let out a breath, his shoulders relaxing.

She set down the plate on a bare spot beside her dad, then gently laid a hand over Chad's.

"I'm sorry." Her words felt so insignificant, so meaningless in the face of the inner ache and turmoil he must have experienced. The way he'd lashed out and declared to "not do pancakes" made perfect sense to her now. If only she'd known, she could have offered a different recipe, refrained from telling the dumb joke.

Then again, he wasn't a thirteen-year-old any longer. His reaction meant he had a lot to work through. And the idea that the man who still held her heart might not be ready made her sad.

* * *

"Okay, time for games!" Darianna said, giving a clap. She had pushed back from the table and Stitches had jumped into her lap again. He gave a little bark, ready to be her second in command.

The dishes had been done, the four of them working as a team while Mrs. Gavras packaged up the leftovers. Chad had worked himself into the routine, placing platters on shelves Athena couldn't reach and even filling the dishwasher to her mom's exacting standards.

If she didn't keep him, despite all the arguments against him, her mom certainly would.

"Grab the tarts. I'll get the plates and napkins," Meddy said to Athena as the group headed to the living room.

Athena took the tray, then turned to Chad, feeling like she should warn him. "It's non-competitive." Lonnie had gotten so into winning that he'd sucked the fun out of game night.

"No, it's cutthroat," Meddy countered, giving him a grin. "And Athena gets worse every year."

"Do not." She shot her a warning look. "And we're nice about our competitive cutthroatedness."

They moved into the living room, selecting seats around the coffee table.

"She has a birthday coming up, so be warned. She's going to get even more crotchety and set in her ways. It's like a stepping stone each year where she—"

Athena gave her a gentle shove. "Shut up."

"Oh, the love," Meddy said, cradling her shoulder like Athena had injured it. "Can't you feel it, Mullens?"

He grinned, seeming to enjoy their sibling banter.

Athena's phone vibrated and, unable to resist the distraction from the warm and fuzzy moment happening around her that was melting her reservations about keeping Chadwick as a boyfriend, she pulled it from the pocket of her cotton skirt. She needed to remember that he was in the process of destroying her career. He'd promised to fix things, and then had vanished. Sure, she'd ghosted him, but she'd have thought he'd at least reach out about a few things he was working on fixing.

She blinked at the preview of the text message from her literary agent, then unlocked her phone to read the entire text.

Her cooking channel had jumped up to thirty-five thousand subscribers. And the stellar pre-order numbers for the cookbook were no longer a rumor. They were high. She might even make bestseller lists.

She waved her phone at Chad. It took him a second to notice. "What's up?"

"Did you do this?" She wanted it to be true, but braced for the truth in case her publisher was the one pulling her butt from the fire.

His expression cautious, Chad took her phone. He read the text, his soft smile growing larger.

"Did you?"

He gave a tiny nod.

"What did you do?"

"This isn't my first rodeo, Tina."

"Speaking of rodeos," Darianna said as she locked the wheels of her chair. "Think you can keep up with us card sharks, Chad?" She grinned at him as she stood, taking the few steps to the couch, looking stronger than she had in weeks.

"Well..." He inhaled slowly as though considering the question while passing Athena's phone back to her. "I think so. I was the Go Fish world champion a few years back. I haven't been training lately, but I'll do my best not to slow everyone down."

Her mom laughed, giving his arm a pat as he sat beside her on the couch. "We're going to expect big things from you now."

Her father and sister had taken the two armchairs, leaving Athena to squeeze between Chad and the armrest. She plopped down, her mind spinning. He *was* fixing things. He'd gone silent because he was working on fulfilling his promise to do that. But not only fixing; he'd been making them better.

Darianna eyed Chad. "Where's your wallet, hon? There's a buy-in."

He blinked, then shifted his weight to reach into his jeans' back pocket.

Athena quickly put a hand on his forearm, stopping him. "She's kidding."

Her mom laughed. "Oh, sweetie. You're no fun."

"Crazy eights?" Neandro suggested.

"You know how to play?" Athena asked Chad. He nodded, confirming a couple of the rules.

Before long, the five of them were whacking cards down on the coffee table and laughing. Chad brought a playful energy to the games that had been missing over the past several weeks, and Athena wanted to freeze time and savor the feeling.

"I needed this," she admitted, leaning back as they finished a round.

Chad glanced over his shoulder, catching her eye. "Me, too."

From across the table, Meddy sent Athena a smug smile. She stuck out her tongue, certain that later on she'd hear from Meddy about how she was an amazing and a wonderful matchmaker.

After tonight, though, Athena wasn't sure if she should keep fighting to keep the validity of her fears at the forefront of her mind, as if they were what mattered most when it came to Chad, or if she should just give up and thank her sister.

CHAPTER 14

Mullens peeled his jersey off over his head and dropped it in a crumpled heap on the locker room's rubber floor. Players were still filtering in from the afternoon practice, and when he looked up, he spotted Athena in the doorway. A sheaf of papers trembled in her grip and she swallowed hard, as though trying to summon the gumption to call the room to attention.

She hadn't always been like that. This was because of him. She didn't know what to expect, didn't know what reaction she might receive. Didn't know if he was going to torch her career or save it.

He'd mended a lot of fences with her over the past several weeks, to the point where she no longer ghosted his text messages, and she'd let him bring her supper in her shop. But he still had work to do. Especially here with the Dragons.

Her soft brown eyes met his, and he saw them harden with an edge of wariness. If he disrespected her, she'd be gone. No more second chances.

And rightly so.

She was a lot more forgiving than he would have been if their roles had been reversed.

"I have a new recipe for everyone," she called, raising her voice to be heard over the din of players. They'd won enough games recently that they were in good spirits, increasing the volume of every locker room interaction.

The chatting quieted, but didn't cease the way it did when the coach addressed them.

"It's super easy and filling," she continued, making her voice louder.

"Hey!" Mullens stood. "Pay attention to Athena!"

"You mean Tina?" Dylan asked with a smirk.

"Shut it, O'Neill."

Athena's eyes had gone wide and she swallowed again. He had a feeling that if she thought she could flee the room without losing face right now, she'd choose that option.

Mullens, still in his skates, towered over his quiet teammates as he made his way past discarded gear to Athena's side.

In his hockey shorts, shoulder and chest pads, he took her stack of recipes.

A chorus of hoots rose in the room as the men waited to see what he'd do with them. Even Athena tensed, the muscles of her neck standing out.

Mullens walked to the room's outer ring, where the lockers and benches were situated. He turned the papers around to read the recipe's name.

"This is a good one." He handed it to a rookie, who crumpled it like Mullens had with the pancake recipe that fateful first day. Mullens cuffed the man upside the head. "Don't be a jerk like me. Show some respect."

He cut a quick glance at Athena and raised his brows, waving the bundle of papers. "Any pro tips for us lugs?"

She blinked, shaking her way out of her stunned silence. "It's a fairly easy recipe. If you have questions, you know where to find me." She turned as if planning to leave, then faced the room again. "Oh, and there are various dietary modifications listed at the bottom for those who need them."

"Hey, Athena?" Mullens called.

She slowly faced him, her expression one of extreme wariness.

"I want to apologize. I know I haven't shown you anywhere near a proper amount of respect in the past. I was a jerk. No excuses. And I'm sorry. I'm going to do better."

She inhaled, her chest expanding, the tension lines in her face smoothing like a reversal of a water drop causing ripples.

Mullens turned back to his task of handing out recipes. "I know y'all probably won't believe me, but I've tried every single one of her recipes from that cookbook she gave us when she joined the team."

"Tried ripping them out of the book, you mean?" Landon muttered, looking at the sheet he'd been given.

"Nope. Cooked them all. Athena knows what she's doing, and in case you haven't figured it out, I'm a giant, disrespectful doofus who she should've taken out back and shot on day one."

"Giant *old* doofus," Leo chirped. The guy was in his late twenties, and not that much younger than the men on the team he called old.

"Yeah, I'm old. Old enough to not act so stupid when trying to catch a woman's attention."

"Dude, you have no game," Dylan said, shaking his head.

"Like you're one to talk. Doesn't Jenny hate you?" Mullens fired back.

Dylan smirked and lifted his brows, making Mullens

wonder if the hate-hate relationship he'd heard about around Sweetheart Creek was actually a pack of lies.

"I hope you'll make him grovel for a *very* long time," Maverick told Athena as he reached for his copy of the recipe.

Mullens made him tug it from his grip, grumbling, "Very funny."

Maverick grinned. "Just trying to be helpful."

"Give her one of your cars, Mullens," Leo suggested. "Then she'll know you're serious about your groveling."

"Women like new cars and trucks," Landon commented, perking up.

"Mullens did let me borrow his Corvette," Athena said, her tone playful.

Mullens. She'd never once called him that. But instead of it feeling like she was putting distance between them, making the interaction impersonal, it felt the opposite. Like he was accepted. All parts of him. From his horrible playboy persona to the guy who was still healing his childhood wounds. From the man who'd disrespected her in front of the team to the one now trying to make amends.

Accepted and forgiven.

He'd never experienced such an overwhelming, surging swell of love.

"Oh-ho!" Dylan crowed. "Mullens has it bad! Look at him!"

He smiled and shook his head. He didn't particularly enjoy being ganged up on by the guys, but if it brought Athena into the team's fold they could tease him for the rest of his life. He might even give them some fodder to keep it going.

"Be careful with him, Athena," Leo said. "He's one of our oldest geezers on the team, and sadly, we still need him."

She smiled at Mullens with such warmth and gratitude

that he ducked his head to hide what was surely a goofy expression.

"I'll keep that in mind, Leo," she said lightly.

"You might want to put him on a soft food diet to help protect his dentures, too." He cackled.

"Hey! Most hockey players have some fake teeth," Mullens protested. As a joke, he lunged at Leo, who laughed and tumbled off his bench.

He wouldn't give up this team for anything.

* * *

Athena straightened up her desk, prepping to head back to Sweetheart Creek. Today, like most weekdays, she'd work the quieter evening shift at the Huckleberry Bookshop before closing up for the night.

She smiled, pressing her palm to her heart as she thought about that earlier moment in the locker room. Her hesitation about forgiving Chad, about possibly dating for real this time, and how he might treat her, had all been laid to rest.

They were both a work in progress, but they were willing to put in the effort.

There was a gentle rapping of knuckles at her open office door, and she turned to see Chadwick Mullens.

Her boyfriend.

He'd changed and showered since she'd last seen him, half an hour ago. He was wearing a crisp, cotton button-up shirt in a deep shade of blue that made his brown eyes seem almost black.

"Got a moment?" he asked, already closing the door behind him.

"What if I don't?" she asked in a sassy tone. She propped a

hand on her hip even though she was suddenly nervous. He was here either to deliver bad news or kiss her.

She really hoped it was a kiss.

"You have to relieve Meddy in about an hour and a half," he said, checking his watch. "I'll keep it quick."

"Are you keeping track of your girlfriend? How possessive of you."

Before he could speak, she made up the distance between them and wrapped her arms around his neck, kissing him deeply, leaving no doubt where she wanted them to be, relationship-wise.

After a long moment they broke apart, resting forehead to forehead.

"So you're officially my girlfriend?" he asked.

She nodded, feeling a sudden shyness.

"No more dodging me? No more being crazy busy?"

"I still have a cookbook to rescue."

He laughed. "It's aiming its way straight up to the top of the bestseller lists. What's to rescue?"

She shrugged.

"You really want three jobs, huh? Hate spending time with me that much?"

"Hey, two of the jobs involve spending a *lot* of time with you."

He kissed her again, slowly and meaningfully, as though they had all the time in the world.

"How about this?" he suggested. "We confess on TV?"

"Confess to what?"

"That we were enemies, and that I did anything and everything to get you riled up. But I don't do that any longer because I finally grew up. Now we're mad about each other instead of mad *at* each other. We can make it cute. You know, capitalize on our relationship to sell the cookbook?"

"That's a bit too cutesy, and goes against your image."

"Maybe it's time for a change. Time to settle down and get the things I truly want."

"And what's that?"

"Love. Marriage. Family. Lots of kids and pets. A real zoo, you know? A house stuffed to the rafters with chaos and people and animals and a million things going on."

Athena blinked at him in surprise. He was serious. He wanted the whole meal deal. And not just that, he wanted to supersize it.

Whatever the man had been doing behind the scenes over the last several weeks to heal his past, the effort seemed to have been well worth it.

"What?" he asked, wrapping his hands around her waist. "You don't want that?"

"I do. It just sounds really busy."

"We both love having full lives."

"True."

"And this kind of hecticness we can do together."

She smiled. She liked his dream.

"You know we haven't actually been on an official date yet." She allowed a finger to lazily trace the edge of the tattoo that dipped under his shirt.

"We can remedy that."

"Good."

Above Chad's collarbone was a branch with a few leaves, a bird that was half-angel. Athena gently tugged at his collar, pulling it downward to take a peek at what was hidden by fabric.

"It's a tree," he said.

She looked up from her survey, meeting his dark eyes, which held a rare invitation to dig deeper. "Why a tree?"

He slipped the top button from its hold, then the next two, pushing the crisp blue fabric aside so she could see more. Distracted by the expanse of muscles, she wondered how long it would be before she saw him without a shirt.

"You wanted to see the tattoo?" he teased. "Hello?"

She sighed and returned her gaze to his tattoo, realizing she'd laid her hands over his and was helping with the buttons.

Tree roots started above his heart, forming a subtle heart shape. The trunk separated into four main branches, stretched from his left shoulder to the midline of his chest. The tattoo was simple, allowing plenty of flesh to show between the fine black lines.

"Your dad..." she said, following one branch to his shoulder. "Your mom..." She traced another with a light finger, causing him to draw a quick breath. Her finger stopped on the highest one which stretched toward the heavens and had the angel-bird lifting off it. "Sister?"

He gave a nod.

The next branch stretched across his chest, was less leafy and appeared unfinished with spots for family to be added close to his heart.

"How many branches do you plan to add over here? Exactly?" she asked playfully, walking her fingers up what must be his own branch.

He chuckled and snagged her hand away. "Depends on my partner and what she wants." His expression was solemn, his gaze locked steadily on hers. There was none of that flirtatiousness she'd come to expect whenever they ventured near anything deep or personal. No deflection. "But as I said earlier. Lots. All the chaos."

Having his attention so solidly on her made Athena want to squirm out from under it, make a joke or lighten the mood. Her question about future branches on his tattoo was heavy with possibility, and his answer was like he was opening a door to the unknown, extending his hand to take hers.

Moments ago everything between them had still felt similar to a dream, fuzzy and uncertain, the edges not yet roughed in.

Forgiveness? Love and a relationship?

She hadn't been 100 percent sure.

But now, seeing his dreams inked on his chest, hearing the question on his lips and the invitation…. Witnessing the opening up, and having those beautiful eyes waiting for her answer….

She cleared her throat. "I want two or three kids. But if I ended up with five, I'd be okay with that."

"Five?" He squinted at her. "How old are you? Is there time?"

She laughed, giving him a light push. He pulled her close, refusing to let her go.

"Seeing the way you're such a sucker for Stitches," she said, "as well as the rumor of how great you were at the Dragons charity's hospital visits, I have a feeling if two people like us got together we could end up with a whole herd of kids. Even more than five."

He smiled softly, the skin around his eyes wrinkling as though he could envision a home and family with her. It would be filled with all the things they'd mentioned, from children and chaos to pets and, above all else, love.

"Yeah," he said, "I could get on board with that."

He pulled at the opening in his shirt, looking down at his chest. "Good thing there's lots of room for additions."

She placed a finger over a spot perfect for a smaller branch. "Maybe one day I'll be on here." Her breath hitched when she realized what she'd said.

But Chad reached over, scooping a pen off her desk. He handed it to her. "Why wait?"

She laughed. "You want me to draw myself onto your family tree?"

Her heart and breath hiccupped like a truck misfiring as she caught the love in his eyes.

"You know, we haven't really known each other that long…" she said hesitantly, lowering the pen. She didn't want to rocket her way up infatuation mountain just to discover she'd completely miscalculated and hit the entirely wrong range.

"I've known you since the day we met." He guided her hand and pen toward his skin. He was watching her, not daring, not pushing, but letting her know it was real for him, and always had been, despite their horrible start.

She licked her lips, wondering if she knew Chad in the way he was suggesting—like an instinct.

"And you know me," he said. "The real me."

"Do I, though?"

"Ask me anything."

"Why were you drinking whiskey at the gala?" A flush heated her face, and she wasn't sure if it was residual anger, frustration over the lack of respect for her rules, or embarrassment for how much his pretend rule-breaking still bothered her.

"Whiskey?" he asked.

"Apple-spiced?"

"Apple, yes. Whiskey, no." His smile slowly warmed. "Juice? Yes."

"No. No, it wasn't." She tossed the pen on her desk and shook her head. Anger rose like bubbles from an underwater air pocket. "I tasted it. And it was…"

Wait. There hadn't been any bite to the droplets she'd tasted. True whiskey surely would have been less sticky and less apple-flavored in such a small amount.

Chad watched her as comprehension dawned.

Her shoulders dropped. "Are you kidding me?" She was just as bad as everyone else—seeing what he put out into the world instead of looking for clues that it was just an illusion.

And he'd been serious outside the rink a few weeks back when he'd vowed he hadn't drunk alcohol since the past summer. She knew he wasn't a liar and yet she hadn't believed him. She hadn't wanted to because it was easier to be scared.

He gave an apologetic shrug.

"Were the other guys drinking whiskey?"

"Not sure."

She sighed. "You're a bad role model."

"I'm trying to do better."

"I know."

"I'm sorry, Athena."

"I know." She wrapped her arms around him again and kissed him slowly, showing him that he was forgiven.

She broke off the kiss. "Give me that pen."

Mullens hadn't quite convinced Athena to draw her name on his chest and add herself to his family tree. He understood her hesitation. It was a pretty bold statement.

She had, however, drawn a heart on the trunk, scrawling their initials inside. He might need to have that permanently inked in place, as he was serious about her being a part of his future. Right now, though, he needed to exercise patience.

While he waited, he would wine and dine her whenever he could, help out with her family and the store, as well as continue to publicly set the record straight about himself, his dietary habits and Athena's upcoming cookbook.

But there was one more little thing he could do for the woman he loved.

"Is everyone ready?" he asked.

"She's coming!" Meddy called from the doorway, quickly unlocking it, then scurrying back to her spot at a table shared with her parents.

Mullens had considered holding this party in Sweetheart

Creek, but he worried that the secret would get out like a toddler trying to hold a wet frog. So instead, he'd rented the Gingerbread Café, which was owned by Dak Morisette, the team's charity manager. He'd reserved the entire place and had instructed Dak to put everything on his tab, from the beautifully decorated gingerbread men the café baked year-round, to the lattes and cocktails, since the cafe was licensed. Not that he was going to drink.

Not unless he somehow ended up engaged to Athena tonight.

He shook his head. He needed to cool his jets. She'd been hurt in the past, not only by Lonnie, but by himself as well. He needed to strengthen her trust in him, and that required time. Lots of time to overwrite all the crappy stuff he'd laid down over the past several months that made him seem untrustworthy.

He hadn't been open about who he really was when they'd first met, because he hadn't been honest about it to himself. But he was working on that, thanks to her. All he could do was continue to work on himself, on them, and hope she understood that the man she knew in her heart was the real Chad Mullens.

But tonight wasn't about him. It was all about her. Meddy had convinced Jenny to take Athena out for a late afternoon snack, pretending she couldn't make it to Athena's birthday supper on the weekend.

There was no birthday supper on the weekend.

Well, maybe there would be, but not the one everyone told her they were holding. Because Mullens had planned a surprise party instead.

Athena's family and friends sat with their backs to the entry, their chatter lulling as Meddy shushed the group.

Mullens took his spot at the counter, facing away from the doorway as well, a giant *Happy Birthday* banner hanging above him. When the bell on the door jingled, he spun to face his girlfriend.

"Surprise!" he called, sliding off the stool and making his way to Athena.

The room echoed with the greeting, people turning to reveal who they were.

Athena's jaw dropped as she recognized her parents, her sister, her cousin Hannah, Daisy-Mae, Cass and Violet, along with their hockey boyfriends, and many more friends from Sweetheart Creek.

"Happy birthday." Mullens pressed a kiss onto her cheek.

"You." She shook her head and poked him in the shoulder, biting her bottom lip as she smiled at the crowded room. "You planned all of this?"

He nodded.

"Thank you." She gave him a hug, and he risked dropping a kiss on her lips in front of everyone. To his surprise, she kissed him back all sexy and slow.

"Hey," she said, breaking the kiss to gaze up at him curiously. "I thought you had a thing tonight. A commercial to film or something?"

"Nope. Just this."

"You're good," she said, patting his chest. "Really good."

"I like to think so."

"By the way, I found a local tattoo artist who's willing to add a little ink." Her hand rested above his tattoo, and an eagle of hope soared through him.

"Yeah? What do you want to add?"

"A name."

"Whose name?"

"Tina. Ever heard of her?"

He tossed his head back and laughed. *Tina.* "Is that her real name? Or is some jerk calling her that to get under her skin?"

"Well, he might be, but she's totally crushing on him."

"Is she?"

"She is. And while the nickname used to annoy her, she now realizes that he was just too afraid to show her how he really felt."

"And how's that?"

"That he loved her?"

"He does?"

"Yes, but it all works out because she loves him, too."

"I should plan surprise parties more often," he whispered when she snuggled in his arms, kissing him lightly and ignoring everyone around them. "Either that or you must have seen the release-day numbers for your cookbook."

"That bestseller has nothing to do with my good mood. It's all about the hunk on the book's cover."

He gave her another kiss, already wishing for a time when he could call her his wife and add many new branches to his tattoo.

"Come on, let the poor man breathe, Athena." Mrs. Gavras tugged her away. "Let's cut the cake."

She was out of her wheelchair today, walking with her cane, her free arm looped through her daughter's, both their smiles bright with love and happiness.

It was a good day.

One of many more to come.

*J*enny Oliver...

Jenny inhaled, shoulders high as she danced with her excitement. She lowered the thick stack of sealed invitations onto the counter.

"This them?" Dylan confirmed.

"This is it."

He grinned. "Ready to send them out?"

"Yeah." It felt like butterflies were doing circuit training in her gut.

"People are going to be shocked." His uncharacteristic grin was full of mischief, but she knew hers was, too. They'd fooled everyone. Even themselves for a little while. "They think we've been joking."

Jenny nodded. "I know!"

"Maybe we should announce our engagement first?"

Jenny laughed. "Why ruin the fun?" She waved the wedding invitations. "Want to go pop them in the mail with me?"

"Yeah. And maybe we should stop at the ring store on the way home and pick out our wedding bands?"

She shrugged, excitement building again. "Why not?"

* * *

Watch for Sugar Cookie Country House next! We'll find out how Jenny and Dylan went from seeming like they were enemies to ready to walk down the aisle.

ACKNOWLEDGMENTS

As always, a huge dose of love goes to my Beta Sisters, my editor, and my HEA error team. You are the best and I appreciate you so very much. Thank you.

A thank you to everyone who patiently weighed in on whether to write " Mullens' " or " Mullens's " as both are technically correct depending on which style guide you prefer to use. It's the small things that trip us writers up the most sometimes!

HOCKEY SWEETHEARTS

Have you read them all?

The Cupcake Cottage

Peach Blossom Hollow

Chocolate Cherry Cabin

The Peppermint Lodge

The Huckleberry Bookshop

Sugar Cookie Country House

The Gingerbread Cafe

A Tiny House Christmas

* * *

There are more stories set in Sweetheart Creek, Texas in these two series:

The Cowboys of Sweetheart Creek, Texas

The Cowboy's Stolen Heart (Levi)

The Cowboy's Secret Wish (Myles)

The Cowboy's Second Chance (Ryan)

The Cowboy's Sweet Elopement (Brant)

The Cowboy's Surprise Return (Cole)

MORE SMALL TOWN ROMANCES BY JEAN ORAM...

Veils and Vows

The Promise (Book 0: Devon & Olivia)

The Surprise Wedding (Book 1: Devon & Olivia)

A Pinch of Commitment (Book 2: Ethan & Lily)

The Wedding Plan (Book 3: Luke & Emma)

Accidentally Married (Book 4: Burke & Jill)

The Marriage Pledge (Book 5: Moe & Amy)

Mail Order Soulmate (Book 6: Zach & Catherine)

Blueberry Springs

Whiskey and Gumdrops (Mandy & Frankie)

Rum and Raindrops (Jen & Rob)

Eggnog and Candy Canes (Katie & Nash)

Sweet Treats (3 short stories—Mandy, Amber, & Nicola)

Vodka and Chocolate Drops (Amber & Scott)

Tequila and Candy Drops (Nicola & Todd)

Champagne and Lemon Drops (Beth & Oz)

The Summer Sisters

Falling for the Movie Star

Falling for the Boss

Falling for the Single Dad

Falling for the Bodyguard

Falling for the Firefighter

ABOUT THE AUTHOR

Jean Oram is a *New York Times* and *USA Today* bestselling romance author. Inspiration for her small town series came from her own upbringing on the Canadian prairies. Although, so far, none of her characters have grown up in an old schoolhouse or worked on a bee farm. Jean still lives on the prairie with her husband, two kids, and big shaggy dog where she can be found out playing in the snow or hiking.

Become an Official Fan:
www.facebook.com/groups/jeanoramfans
Instagram: www.instagram.com/author_jeanoram
Facebook: www.facebook.com/JeanOramAuthor
Shop: shop.jeanoram.com
Newsletter: www.jeanoram.com/signup
Website & blog: www.jeanoram.com